# BLUE COLLAR BILLIONAIRE

AMY ANDREWS

Boldwood

First published in Great Britain in 2025 by Boldwood Books Ltd.

Copyright © Amy Andrews, 2025

Cover Design by Colin Thomas

Cover Images: Colin Thomas and iStock

A CIP catalogue record for this book is available from the British Library.

Paperback ISBN 978-1-83617-982-5

Large Print ISBN 978-1-83617-983-2

Hardback ISBN 978-1-83617-981-8

Trade Paperback ISBN 978-1-80656-035-6

Ebook ISBN 978-1-83617-984-9

Kindle ISBN 978-1-83617-985-6

Audio CD ISBN 978-1-83617-976-4

MP3 CD ISBN 978-1-83617-977-1

Digital audio download ISBN 978-1-83617-978-8

This book is printed on certified sustainable paper. Boldwood Books is dedicated to putting sustainability at the heart of our business. For more information please visit https://www.boldwoodbooks.com/about-us/sustainability/

Boldwood Books Ltd, 23 Bowerdean Street, London, SW6 3TN

www.boldwoodbooks.com

*To nerd girls everywhere and the hot guys who dig them.*

# 1

## HOLLY

There are three things I need this morning. A hot shower, a warm bed, and twelve hours of solid sleep. But the universe, which takes frequent delight in thwarting me, isn't playing ball.

It delivers on the hot shower, but I'm now freezing my ass off in my apartment because the heating refuses to bend to my will. That's going to make the sleeping bit impossible. The blinding fuzz of white outside my window confirms there's still a blizzard going on out there.

I'll be a freaking popsicle after a few hours.

I bang the clunky old radiator with a wrench a few more times, hoping for some kind of miracle. That's how tired I am.

'I should have gotten a job in California,' I tell the freezing metal. 'There aren't any blizzards in California. There's sun and sand. And drinks with little umbrellas. But no... I chose the Rocky Mountains.' I smash the wrench against the radiator again. 'For the skiing. Which I never get time to do anyway.'

God. I'm so tired. I've been working all night and I just want to crawl into my bed, burrow under the covers, and not reappear until the blizzard blows itself out. Or I'm back on shift again in three days.

Whatever comes first.

But now I'm going to have to go downstairs and throw myself at the mercy of my building super. Ordinarily I wouldn't have a problem with taking my lack of heating to Bob. He's been manager of the apartment block for a decade.

I've only been here for two of those but he's a nice old guy in his late sixties who can fix anything, and nothing's ever too much trouble.

But Bob's off on his annual trek to Reno for two months where he meets up with some old military buddies. They play the tables in between visiting the all-you-can-eat buffet. I don't think he's ever had much of a win because, let's face it, while this building is serviceable, it ain't exactly the Ritz.

And if he'd won big, surely he'd retire somewhere nice where he didn't have to be on call to eighty apartments every minute of the day, especially during a blizzard.

That job currently, however, belongs to Bob's only living relative. The son of a distant cousin long deceased who has just moved back to the area. Apart from their supernatural ability to fix things, there's absolutely no family resemblance between Bob and Danny Colton.

Where Bob is paunchy and moon-faced, Danny is ripped, with a face that's as chiselled as the rest of him. Even his name conjures up dusty cowboys and pistols at dawn. If cowboys had tattoos. Because he has plenty of them decorating his chest and arms and neck.

He's also irritatingly cocky.

The guy only has to look at me and I feel like a stammering teenager again. The kind with braces and no breasts. And he knows it. He has that smug smile that tells me he's used to women's brains melting as he walks by. Which is especially irritating for someone like me, who prides herself on her brains and her cool.

I'm an ER doctor, for crying out loud. I don't like to brag, but I'm not exactly dumb. And you wouldn't believe some of the shit that goes down at work that never ruffles a feather. But one slight uptilt of Danny the drummer's mouth, and bang!

I drop a hundred IQ points.

Yeah. He's a drummer. Of course. Plays in a rock band by night, hibernates during the day, in between callouts for leaky taps, broken appliances, and collecting the rent – or whatever an apartment super does. Except for when he's practising. Which always seems to be the days I'm trying to sleep after a night shift.

Always.

I've had to pound on his door to tell him to shut up several times this past couple of weeks. He always does, but not before he's answered the door looking like God's gift to vaginas in jeans and nothing else but that stupid, sexy smile. It keeps me awake for freaking hours afterwards.

I've lost a lot of sleep since Danny Colton came to stay. And lack of sleep makes me cranky. I've been cranky for the past few weeks.

I'm really freaking cranky now.

Throwing the wrench on the ground, I dash to my bedroom, resigned to my fate. But I have to bundle up first. We'll no doubt end up in the basement, and it'll be subzero down there. My long johns might be just right for bed, but I'm going to need more layers.

I climb into sweatpants and thick socks, shoving my feet in my Uggs as I pull a long-sleeved Henley over my head and follow it with a turtleneck sweater, then my puffy navy-blue jacket. Reaching for my pink knit beanie with the pompom on top, I pull it down to my ears, haphazardly shoving strands of my hair underneath.

It's not very fashionable but it's warm and my grandmother knitted it for me the winter before she died in a car crash, which devastated the entire family. It makes me feel close to her and reminds me why I'm busting my ass working and studying all hours of the day and night.

Finally, I yank the duvet off the bed and throw it around my shoulders like some kind of kick-ass cape. It's down so it'll keep me warm in the basement. Plus it totally hides my body, which is a win-win as far as I'm concerned. I need some kind of shield against the way Danny looks at me.

Like he wants to play doctor. The kind of doctor that specialises in sexual healing.

Shutting my eyes against the temptation of that image, I stalk out of the bedroom. As I sweep past the coffee table, the bulk of the duvet brushes against the stack of study papers I have waiting for me, and they fall to the floor.

'Fabulous,' I mutter, but keep walking. If the room was warmer I'd probably give a shit. I will later tonight when I have to get them all back into order again. But they are so not my priority at the moment.

Getting this place warm is my priority. And for that, I need Danny Colton.

Damn it.

\* \* \*

As it always does, the number sixty-nine confronts me as I shuffle to Danny's door. I guess it's not his fault – this is Bob's place, after all – and somebody has to be apartment sixty-nine. But it figures the guy who looks like he knows all the sexual positions in the Kama Sutra, and probably a few that aren't, would end up here.

Muffled music leaks around the door, and for some reason it pisses me off. I'm tired and freezing my ass off, and he's having a... house party. The thought he might be entertaining someone in there makes me even more irritated.

I never get the chance to entertain. At twenty-seven, I have several years to go before I become an attending. I work eighty-hour weeks and study whatever hours are left. I barely have time to eat and sleep, and forget about anything recreational like shopping and reading and seeing my parents. I barely maintain friendships past people I work with.

Relationships? Sex? Pfft. I can't remember the last time I had sex.

Hell, I can't even remember the last time I was in the mood for sex. I'm bankrupt on time and drowning in student loan debt – there's nothing groovy-sexy-times about that.

My crankiness dials up another notch.

Slipping my hand out from under all my layers, I knock on the door. The cool kiss of air on my fingers makes me grateful for the snugness of the duvet. The tip of my nose is cold, and I don't have to look at it to know it's red. The door remains stubbornly closed, and I grit my teeth and pound my fist against the wood.

A beat passes. Then another. The door opens on a waft of warm air and Bruce Springsteen, and I'm looking up into eyes as warm and blue as tropical waters. Suddenly, my vagina – yeah, I call body parts by their proper names; it's a doctor thing – remembers exactly how long it's been since it's seen any action.

Seven months, twenty-two days. And it wasn't very good.

I came home after to finish the job. The guy – a travelling medical rep – really could have done with reading an anatomy textbook or two. Not that familiarity with anatomy had helped my long-ago ex who had been studying to be a surgeon.

Danny's laugh interrupts my walk down crappy-sex lane. Deep dimples bracket either side of his mouth as his eyes take a tour of my Rudolph-nosed,

Yeti-like appearance. I hunch into the duvet a little more, feeling about as attractive as the dirty slush that's churned up by snow ploughs.

He, on the other hand, glows with warmth and vitality and sex appeal, stretching the shoulder seams of his T-shirt. Green and black tattoos with splashes of colour cling to his biceps, and wings of some description flare either side of his neck. Soft denim hugs low on his hips and cups every single thing south. His dirty blond hair is a little on the shaggy side, as is his jaw stubble. He's a tropical mirage, and I want to reach out and touch him just to see if he really does exist.

His tour of my bulky form complete, he shoves his shoulder against the doorjamb and lazily raises an eyebrow. If the man was any more laid back, he'd be horizontal.

'Dr Vincent.'

Danny says *doctor* the way most men say *baby*. It's hot enough to make every single thing I have on at the moment mentally fall off my body in anticipation. I can only imagine how many groupies he must have. I bet my medical degree the people who've been with this man never have to go home and finish the job.

My crankiness reaches boiling point. 'My heat isn't working.'

His gaze flicks up and down my body again, his mouth quirking sexily. 'I figured.'

I blink. Is that it? He figured? Did he think I was standing here dressed like the Abominable Snowman just to inform him of my current heating situation? Or lack of, as the case may be. A nerve jumps under my left eye, and I quell the urge to still it with my finger.

'Look... I'm tired. I've worked all night and I'd like to go to sleep now but, in case you haven't noticed, there's a blizzard happening out there, and my apartment is freezing, and I have no desire to die of hypothermia in my sleep.'

He grins, flashing those dimples one more time. He actually grins. 'You doctors.' He shakes his head and makes a tsking sound. 'Always with the big words.'

My nipples love that tsking sound. They're under a billion layers of clothing and bedding, yet still, they perk right on up as if his lips have tsked directly against them.

Traitors.

Annoyed at this development, I cross my arms. Not that Danny can possibly see their reaction to his teasing, but I haven't entirely ruled out the prospect that the man has been gifted with X-ray vision along with his many other attributes.

Either way, my erect nipples are none of his business.

I smile sweetly. 'I'll try to keep my words to one syllable in future.'

Not remotely insulted, the smile hovers on his lips. 'It'll probably be an easy fix.' He pushes off the doorjamb. 'Come in.'

Ordinarily, I would have stayed on his doorstep. A smart woman like me knows to keep the hell away from temptation, and Danny Colton is temptation wrapped up in glittery paper and tied in a big red bow. But it's warm in there and the corridor is cold, and I'm too tired to fight biology.

I take a step into his apartment. It's toasty, but I barely register it, bracing myself instead for the urge to strip off my clothes and demand that Danny do me – which in all honesty is my main concern about crossing his threshold. When it doesn't happen, I relax. When I realise he's disappeared somewhere, I relax a little more.

Of course my nipples are still misbehaving. I tweak them under all those layers in an effort to settle them down. It doesn't help. If anything, they get stiffer, and things stir high and deep between my legs like I've somehow just tweaked my own G spot.

Great – I'm turning myself on. In the lair of a sex god. I must be really tired.

'You stay here.'

I startle as Danny reappears suddenly and pull my hands off my breasts in case he can see what's happening beneath the duvet. He's put on a hoodie, which he's zipped up, and he's carrying a large rectangular leather tool bag in one hand, which I know belongs to Bob.

'I won't be long,' he continues, oblivious to my turmoil. Or at least I hope he is.

'Oh no.' I shake my head. 'I'm coming with you.'

'Doc.'

My breath hitches. He hasn't called me that before, and man... it does funny things to my equilibrium. It shouldn't. It's not like I don't get called it about a hundred times a shift, but it sounds like a cute nickname on his lips. And that's all kinds of titillating.

'I have to go to the basement.' He says it slowly, like maybe I'm the one out of us that needs small syllables. 'It'll be cold as a witch's tit down there.'

I blink at his profanity. I don't use those kinds of words myself. Usually. Not that I'm offended when it comes from others. Lord knows, I've been sworn at by patients too many times to count. It's just that my mother always told me cussing was for people who had poor vocabularies.

A shame she never told me what a huge turn-on it could be.

'I know. Hence...' I look down my body to indicate the reason I'm dressed as if I'm wearing every article of clothing in my closet is because of the basement. 'If it's a quick fix, then you can teach me how to do it. That way I won't need to belt on your door every time my heating decides to go hinky.'

No way do I want to rely on Danny freaking Colton any more than I have to. And why should I bother Bob in future if it's something simple?

'You want to get busy with my tools?'

He's laughing at me, but I refuse to rise to the bait. I have no doubt he can flummox me with sexual banter, especially given how tired I am, but he can't if I don't engage. 'I've operated on people's brains and hearts with highly complex surgical instruments.' I might be in the ER now, but I've done my surgical rotation. 'I'm pretty sure I can handle a screwdriver.'

He smiles bigger. 'Well, this I gotta see.'

He indicates for me to precede him, and I sweep out of the room as regally as I can in my floral duvet and pink pompom beanie. The door clicks shut behind me as I turn in the direction of the stairs.

'We have to take the elevator.' His voice stops me in my tracks. 'The damp down there has rotted the wood in the stairs. I put my foot through one last night and nearly fell on my ass all the way down. I've cordoned them off. I'll fix them as soon as the storm stops and I can go get the stuff.'

Turning back in his direction, I try not to think about Danny down in the basement, a tool belt slung low on his hips, getting all covered in sawdust as he repairs the treads. His back view doesn't help. His ass in those jeans is like something out of an anatomy textbook – two tight, taut buttocks – and I want to strip him just to admire the musculature.

A great set of glutes is a magnificent thing.

I blink at the direction of my thoughts. What am I doing? Has my brain completely checked out? This isn't the set of a porn film. I must be in the delirious stage of sleep deprivation. I give myself a mental shake and drag my gaze off his ass, going wide-screen now. The ease of his swagger as he ambles down the corridor with those perfect glutes is suddenly irritating, and I remember the other thing I find irksome about him.

The man never seems to be in a hurry to get anywhere.

Like he has all the time in the world and the world will just wait for him, anyway. For someone who's always busy, it's really freaking annoying.

There are never enough hours in my day to fit everything in. At work, there's rarely a moment to recoup before the next thing comes along, even in the middle of the night. And if there is a weird lull, I fill it with paperwork. I eat on the run, see patients on the run, take calls on the run. Hell, I rarely even get to go to the restroom.

So yeah. I really, really resent this guy for his sexy, what's-your-rush-baby swagger.

He halts at the elevator, and I shuffle past him to stand on the other side of the doors. The hallway is silent, its usual Monday morning buzz eerily absent. No one is going to work today. Everyone from the head honcho meteorologist to the police chief to the mayor has urged people to stay indoors until the blizzard blows over.

The elevator dings and the doors slide open to reveal a sparkling, spotless interior. The cleaning service would have done their thing last night and, what with the weather and all, I doubt anybody's ridden in it since. Danny indicates that I should precede him, so I do.

It's a large space – registered for twenty people – and warm. Or maybe that's just the heat flowing to my cheeks and buzzing through my thighs as I immediately claim the furthest corner right at the back. Danny smirks as he saunters inside and plants that ass against the wooden railing nearest the buttons, obviously amused by my distance.

Pushing the button that says B, he turns his head to look at me. 'Going down?'

I cock a sarcastic eyebrow at his suggestive remark. At least, I hope it's sarcastic and not a come-closer-and-say-that eyebrow my traitorous body has formed without my consent. He just smiles as the doors close, but holy moly... my head is full of images of going down.

Of me going down on him. Him going down on me.

The elevator shrinks suddenly, and he seems to fill it with his sheer physicality. I feel the pull of him from a few feet away and grip the handrail behind me to stop myself from edging closer as the numbers tick down from six.

So freaking slow.

Five. Four. Three. Two—

The elevator suddenly shudders to a stop, and the movement jolts through my knees. The lights go out and the alarm starts to ring as the emergency lighting flickers on. It's subdued, but there's enough of a glow so we're not in total darkness. I press a hand to my chest to still my accelerating heart, but it's too late; it's already in my throat.

'The electricity must have gone out.'

He says it as calm and laid back as the rest of him, and I want to scream. I'm tired, I need my bed, and the bell is blaring like a freaking huge warning. To me, probably. I do not want to be trapped in an elevator with Mr Going Down for an indeterminate period of time.

The man looks like he knows how to pass the time.

He pins me with his gaze, his dimples deepening as his slow, lazy smile grows. 'Whatever will we do?'

# 2

## DANNY

I don't know why my very existence seems to annoy the crap out of Holly Vincent, but it does. Always has. Since that first day she banged on my door a couple of weeks ago and yelled at me to stop playing my drums, I've had a hard-on for her.

She was covered up that day as well, in some kind of fluffy-looking dressing gown that went from her neck to her toes, and there'd been a blanket mark on her face. But her dark hair had tumbled all around her face and she'd glared at me with her weird amber eyes, and I knew I wanted her.

Knew I was going to have her, too.

Just maybe not today, as she glowers at me from the back corner of the elevator, wrapped up like Kenny from *South Park*.

'I cannot be stuck in this elevator.'

Her voice is 100 per cent pissed off as she stalks towards me, the duvet she has swathed around herself sweeping the ground. I love seeing that spark in her eyes. The spark she had that first day she yelled at me. It's perversely pleasing to see Little Miss Cool all fired up, especially considering how much time I've spent wondering just how fired up she might get between the sheets.

Of course, it's only me she's cool with. She's a regular ray of sunshine with the other residents. Opening doors, carrying bags, putting up vaccination clinic flyers and always giving free medical advice.

'You're not one of those panicky women, are you?'

I ask because I know it's going to piss her off even further, and she doesn't disappoint. She stops in front of me and glares.

'Do I look like the panicking type to you?'

Her voice lowers but it's still vehement enough to be heard over the alarm. And there's a vibrato to it, which I'm fairly sure comes from rage rather than panic.

I bet she's awesome when she's angry-fucking.

'I'm just sayin'.' I inject a little redneck into my accent because it seems to piss her off even more when I act dumb. She doesn't need to know that I graduated business school. 'There's no need to worry. It's a big elevator, and there's only two of us. We're not going to run out of air or anything.'

She rolls her eyes, and I suppress a smile. 'I know that. I have a medical degree.'

I laugh. Some guys might be insulted by a woman lording it over them because she thinks he's a little lacking in the brains department. Not me. I've seen her checking me out the times our paths have crossed, and I didn't get to twenty-nine without knowing when a woman is interested.

She's not as immune to me as she wants me to think.

Sure, she's all haughty and brainy and you-can't-touch-this, and she looks at me like I'm too blue-collar for her. But sometimes a woman likes a bit of rough – any drummer can tell you that – and I'm happy to be her piece of rough.

I'm happy to be whatever the fuck she wants.

'Of course, if the building catches on fire, we're toast.'

She gives me a not-funny look. 'Have I mentioned how tired I am?'

'Right.' I turn to the panel next to the buttons and pull open the door. There's a phone with *emergency use only* emblazoned on the handle and a button for the alarm. I pick up the phone and push the button, and the noise cuts off as abruptly as it started.

Silence falls, and I swear I hear Holly sigh.

The phone is ringing in my ear as I settle back against the wall again, and I watch her surreptitiously out the corner of my eye. A female voice chirps a greeting and between the two of us, we quickly ascertain that this elevator isn't going anywhere in a hurry, given the demands on emergency services at present.

I hang up, and Holly says, 'Well?'

It's impatient as hell, and I try not to be either insulted or turned on by her eagerness to be out of here. I know she wants to be back in her bed. But I also know there's more than that going on. I know she doesn't want to be trapped in here with me because she has a thing for me. And she's frightened she might act on it.

A situation I certainly wouldn't object to. We do have several hours to kill, after all. My dick is already on board with the idea.

'They don't know when they'll be able to get here. Probably not for a few hours.' She opens her mouth to interrupt, but I don't give her an opening. 'Services are already badly stretched. There are actual real life-and-death emergencies going on out there.'

I don't need to tell her that, of course. As she's fond of saying – she's an ER doctor. She's probably been dealing with them all night. 'Two healthy people stuck in a large elevator for a few hours are not a priority.'

She huffs out a sigh. 'Yeah.' It's the most dejected *yeah* I've ever heard.

'But they know, and they'll get to us when they can, and she's going to keep us up to date. And if the electricity comes back on and the elevator starts working again, she wants to know so she can cross us off her list.'

Holly nods, then slides down the back wall until she's sitting. She bends her legs up, or at least I think she does. It's hard to tell under all that bulk.

'Sorry.' I don't know why I'm apologising. But she looks exhausted. Even in the reduced lighting I can see the tautness of the skin around her eyes. I hadn't slept last night either. But I'd just been banging drums all night, not saving lives.

She drops her head back against the wall. 'It's not your fault.'

'You have to work tonight?'

'Nope.' Her head rocks back and forth along the wall as she shakes it. Her eyes flutter closed. 'Three days off.'

Which is probably just as well. I doubt she could get in tonight, anyway. For damn sure city officials won't want her out there on the roads trying.

Covering the distance between us, I too slide down the wall to sit beside her, leaving a few feet between us. Her eyes, big and amber, blink open. 'What are you doing?'

'Sitting.' I smile because the answer obviously irritates her.

'There's plenty of wall space.'

'I thought you might like to lie down.' I pat my thighs. 'Horizontal is always better, and I'm reliably informed they make a very good pillow.'

She gives a soft snort and somehow, even though her head only comes to my shoulder, she manages to look down her nose at me.

'I bet you have been.'

I laugh. 'Just sayin'.'

She shuts her eyes again. 'I'm a shift worker. I don't need to be horizontal. I can sleep standing up. I can sleep at a desk or lying on a hard, cold floor. I could sleep hanging upside down like a bat if I had to.'

That's an image I don't need in my head right now. The things I could do to her in that position... 'Have it your way.'

But she doesn't answer, and, when I look closer, her lips have parted and there's a slackness to them that tells me she's fallen asleep. Impressive. She really can go to sleep anywhere. Even, apparently, mid-conversation.

It only takes a minute, though, before she starts to sag and slide towards me. She jerks briefly awake a couple of times, muttering as she rights herself, but eventually even that's beyond her, and she slides all the way down.

I grab her before she face-plants into the floor and shuffle my ass towards her a little, sticking my leg under her head. She makes no protest, just squirms for a bit once she's fully horizontal, her head shifting around into my lap. My cock appreciates her subconsciousness trying to find a position of comfort, but cracking wood is hardly appropriate in the situation.

I hold my breath and think of plunging my dick into a snow drift until she stops wriggling and relaxes into sleep. I have no idea why it's so damn interested, anyway. She looks like a giant pig in a blanket. Not one curve or flash of skin exposed, just her pink little face amidst the lumpy duvet, a ratty pair of Uggs, and a pink pop-pom cap.

So I ignore my idiot dick and close my eyes, my head falling back against the wall behind. I could use some sleep too, and it's that or get wound up about a sleeping woman I have no intention of touching anyway.

She wants me. I want her. And for damn sure I'm going to explore that a little more while we're both stuck in here if I get the time. But now, she needs to sleep, and I'm going to be the perfect fucking gentleman and let her.

\* \* \*

'Oh God, I'm so sorry.'

I'm woken by a whispered, scandalised apology, a quick intake of breath and a sudden lightness in my lap. Holly sits bolt upright and blinks at me, owl-like, from within her bundle of covers, like she can't remember how she ended up in my lap.

Her face is flushed but I'm not sure if it's from sleep or embarrassment or heat. It's stuffy in here now, the air warm. She must be overheating like crazy.

'What time is it?'

She looks around as I dig my phone out of my hoodie pocket. I can't believe it's not even been a full hour since she drifted off. 'Nine-thirty.'

'Is that all?' When I nod, she seems to consider it for a few seconds, then pushes the duvet off her shoulders to reveal a puffy jacket and some sweat-pants. 'It's hot in here.' She grabs the rail and hauls herself to her feet, walking to the door. 'Is it hot in here or is it just me?' She turns back and looks at me for my answer.

'It's a little stuffy,' I admit. 'But you are trussed up like you're about to head up a dogsled team.'

She looks at herself and grimaces. 'You're right.'

Unzipping her jacket with one hand, she pulls the beanie off with the other. I open my mouth to protest – she looks damn cute in that beanie – but then her dark hair tumbles down over her shoulders, and the heat that left my groin when Holly removed herself from my lap surges back.

Not content to stop there, she shrugs out of her jacket and tosses it aside. The sweater she has on also goes as she toes off her Uggs. Suddenly, she's a lot less bulky. There's just a ribbed Henley that moulds to her tits and her stomach and maybe something else underneath, but not a bra.

I don't need to be an expert in boobs – although I am – to see that.

'That's better,' she announces.

I concur. 'Don't stop on my account.'

She blinks like it's just occurred to her she's performed a bit of a strip tease. Colour suffuses her cheeks, and this time the flush has nothing to do with the stuffiness of the elevator. She folds her arms and does that looking down her nose thing again.

If she thinks she's hiding her tits from me, she's wrong – the pull of her shirt across them makes me salivate. I want to put my mouth on them so bad my lips burn with the urge.

'I think it's far enough.'

Oh no. Not nearly far enough. But we'll see. I laugh at her primness, though. I'm beginning to like how she condescends to me, which is about as fucked up as it gets. My balls ache with how much it turns me on.

She ignores my laughter as she gathers the duvet, gives it a shake, and spreads it over the floor. It takes up about half of the space, and she sits on top of it but against the opposite wall. Smart, smart woman.

'Why do you do that?'

Her question surprises me as she glares across the space between us, stretching her legs out in front of her. Her socks are stripy, her thighs shapely. Her arms are crossed, and there's a little V drawing her eyebrows together.

'Why do I do what?'

I know what she's asking, but I really want to see if she'll say it. If she'll put it out there. Too many times these past few weeks she's walked away from the invitation in my eyes. Is she going to tackle it now?

She raises her chin. 'Look at me like you... know me.'

Okay. She is going there. My dick stirs at the thought; my pulse quickens. Does she think her forthrightness will scare me off? That I'll back down now she's telling me she knows my game? 'Because I do know you.'

She shakes her head. 'No, you don't.'

Her denial is swift and vehement. 'Fair enough.' My pulse drums slowly through my groin, the blood thick through my veins as I raise my hands in surrender. 'But I know some things about you.'

She looks away, her hands falling to her sides to smooth the duvet cover. Her tits shift nicely, and I look my fill while her attention is elsewhere.

'I know that I annoy you.' She doesn't say anything, just keeps working the duvet. 'I know you don't want to want me.' Her hands halt. 'But you do, anyway.'

Her fingers pluck at the duvet now. Her breathing roughens; I can hear it from here. 'That's not true.'

She's lying and we both know it, but I'm fine with a little denial. 'It's okay,' I soothe. 'I understand. I'm not your type. But sexual attraction doesn't always come in a neatly wrapped box. Sometimes we want what we want and there's no rhyme or reason to it.'

Her hands stop again, and her eyes lift to mine. Our gazes lock. 'I don't have time for... dalliances.'

Christ, even the way she says *dalliances* makes me horny. So prim. I want
that proper mouth wrapped around my cock doing improper things. 'Doc.' I
smile and shake my head at her. 'You need to make time.'

'I'm fine.'

She tosses her head, and I almost groan as her boobs bounce to the
movement. I quirk my eyebrow in mock inquiry, just to see her spark up. She
does.

'I am.'

I shake my head slowly. 'You're pissed off all the time.'

'Only at you.'

I laugh. Touché. But she bristles even more at my amusement.

'I'm only ever... cranky at you.'

'Cranky?' This woman is hysterical. 'God, I love your primness. You can't
even say the words. Can't say Danny Colton pisses me off. It's okay to say it, you
know.'

'Gee.' She smiles at me, her teeth gritted. 'Thanks for the permission.'

'It might even help.'

'Help?'

'Loosen you up a bit.'

'Why? So I can schlep around shirtless all day, keeping my neighbours
awake with my drum practice?'

'I'm all for you schlepping around shirtless.'

She folds her arms. Her amber eyes glow in the low light. 'You're doing it
again.'

I smile. 'Pissing you off?'

'You think all this casual cussing makes you some kind of... cool dude?'

I throw my head back and laugh this time. Is she kidding? I'm a drummer.
I'm already pretty cool. But I don't point this out. I change tack. 'Your momma
teach you cussing was a sin?'

'Didn't yours?'

I ignore her question. 'I suppose she thinks the F word sends you straight
to hell?' I wonder how sick it is on a scale of one to ten for me to want to hear
such a dirty word coming from such a prim mouth?

Her eyes widen. Just a little, but I notice it. I notice everything about her.
The slight roughness in her breath as it slides in and out of her magnificent
mouth; the way her toes curl inside her socks. I definitely notice how she

crosses one ankle over the other and slides a hand into the valley where her thighs meet, right up high, snuggled into her crotch.

Is she getting hot just from talking about cussing? From the mention of the F word? Is it starting to hurt between those legs?

'I'm pretty sure my momma doesn't spend any of her time thinking about the F word.'

Her voice is high and breathy, but she looks at me, her eyes glowing with defiance, her chin in the air. I say, 'Like mother like daughter, huh?' just to rile her up even more.

Her lips flatten. 'I told you before, I don't have time for—'

'Dalliances.' I grin as I complete her sentence, then I shake my head at her. Such a waste. 'How long's it been since you had an orgasm, Doc?' She goes to speak, and I hold up my hand. 'With another human being. Not one you've given to yourself.'

Her face flushes so fast and so bright its glow practically lights up the whole elevator.

'Ahhh... I see... You don't do that either, do you?' I laugh, not out of callousness but out of wonder.

This woman... so much I can teach her.

'I told you already.' Her gaze drops to her lap, where her thumb is brushing back and forth over the top of her thigh. 'I don't have time.'

'It only takes a minute.'

Her eyes flick up, but not all the way – they come to rest on my crotch. It's too dim in here to see I'm sporting full wood, but my dick feels the intensity of her gaze like a giant wet tongue licking it from root to tip. 'For guys, maybe.'

Okay. That does it. Getting stuck in an elevator with this woman today has obviously been predestined. If anyone needs to learn the power of her own body, it's Holly Vincent. If anyone needs a good orgasm, it's her.

This is her lucky day.

'What if I told you I could give you one now? Fast and easy. No strings.'

Her breath hitches, and she blinks. Her mouth drops open. I try not to think about all the things I could do to that mouth. She draws her knees up. 'That's... preposterous,' she splutters, but it's too late; I already heard that little hitch. 'If you think I'm getting naked in here with you then—'

'You can stay fully clothed,' I interrupt.

'What?'

'So will I.'

She stares at me like I've gone crazy, and for a moment I think maybe I have, too. I want to see her naked so fucking bad.

'I won't kiss you. Hell, I'll barely even touch you. I just need my hand.' I hold it up and wiggle the fingers. 'That's all.'

I can settle for her wet and slippery against my fingers, if that's what it takes to touch her. And hearing my name bounce off these walls as she comes her brains out won't exactly be a hardship, either. She stares at my fingers as if hypnotised for a beat before giving herself a shake.

'No, thanks. I have no desire to be bragged about at your next jam session.'

Her loaded dismissal is a barb to my chest. I do not brag about women. That's just plain disrespectful – my momma taught me *that*. My gaze locks with hers, and I shake my head very slowly, very deliberately.

'What happens in the elevator stays in the elevator.'

Her ragged breathing is loud in the silence that grows as her legs slide down to stretch out in front again. Her hand snakes between her thighs as she chews on her bottom lip.

She's actually thinking about it...

My cock is hard as stone, the teeth of my zipper biting into the taut flesh as her head turns and she stares at the doors. Oh, yeah baby, she wants it.

'They could... come at any moment.'

'No.' The only person coming here is her. I hope. 'Not for a couple of hours.' I throw her one of my most irritatingly cocky smiles. 'I could give you a dozen in that time.'

Her nostrils flare, but she shakes her head. 'This is... ridiculous.'

She's so, so close. I can tell she wants to say yes. The flush in her cheeks betrays her arousal, her curiosity. I fold my arms at my sides like wings and flap. 'Bok. Bok. Bok.'

She purses her lips, obviously unimpressed, but there's a lot of thinking going on behind those pretty eyes. 'So you just... give me an... orgasm... and that's it?'

I sincerely fucking hope not, but if that's the way she wants it. 'Yep.' I nod. 'I put my hand down your pants—' Her eyes widen, and I smile. She is so ripe for this I swear I can already smell how wet she is. 'And I make you come so hard you'll see angels. And then I'll take my hand out and sit back over here and we can... talk about the weather.'

But if I play my cards right, she's going to want a hell of a lot more, like seeing how much harder she can come on my cock. 'Whaddya say, Doc?' I waggle my fingers again.

She swallows. 'I... I...' But her eyes are on my hand and they're all jittery, and her chest is rising and falling rapidly, and I have her. I know I do.

I reach over, grab her ankle, and yank.

# 3

## HOLLY

Oh dear God. I'm going to hell. Like the really bad hell that's below all the other hells. I lay flat on the floor and don't move as Danny crawls on his hands and knees towards me. I should be righting myself. Telling him no. Telling him absolutely not.

How will I ever face him again?

But my tongue sticks to the roof of my mouth, and I just lay there, my heart trying to beat its way out of my chest, my gaze glued to his slow, measured prowl. I want it. I want this. Want him.

I want him to put his hand down my pants and make me come.

I absolutely believe if any man can make me see angels, it's him. Even though it's such a sacrilegious thing to think, which is another reason I'm going to hell, but damn... the man has a way with words.

*What happens in the elevator stays in the elevator.*

More great words. Their permissiveness echoes through my head and whispers in my ear as his body looms over mine, and I'm too far gone to do anything other than follow their lead. It's like I checked my morals at the door when I stepped in the elevator.

His knees are either side of my hips now, although they don't touch, and his hands are planted either side of my shoulders, his arms straight, his body held at arm's length from mine as he stares down at me and I am caught in the warm, blue heat of his gaze.

My pulse flutters erratically at my temple, pounds hard in my chest, and throbs heavy between my legs.

Not taking his eyes from mine, he lifts his right hand. It hovers down my body, and I suppress the urge to arch my back so it makes contact on its way to its destination. My nipples are so hard they feel as if they're about to pop right off.

His hand lands softly just above the drawstring waist of my sweatpants. I gasp as my stomach muscles contract. I can't stop it, can't call it back, and he just smiles.

Like he knows.

And I hate him a little bit, but I need him to keep going.

He does, his hand burrowing beneath the layers of fleece and long johns and underwear until it skims against bare flesh, and I shiver and cry out and really do arch my back now as his fingers slide against the aching flesh between my legs.

'Is that where it hurts, Doc?' His gaze is like a missile locked on mine. I want to shut my eyes, to look away, but I am mesmerised. And he knows that, too. 'Is that where you need me?'

'Yes.'

A pent-up sob falls from my lips as his fingers find my clitoris and start to tease. My hips lift, circle to the motion of his hand. My heart crashes against my rib cage, and I'm panting, and he's barely started.

'Oh yes,' he whispers, his eyes burning bright. 'I knew you'd be this wet for me.'

Two fingers find my entrance, and he shoves inside me, and I cry out and grab his arm. The edges of my world start to fold in on themselves.

'So tight.' He draws them slowly out. 'So wet.' He pushes them slowly in.

I can barely breathe for the sensations swamping me. I want to shut my eyes, but I can't. I can't look away from him, from the way he's looking at me, like he's getting off on it as much as I am.

'You know what you should do now?' he asks as his fingers slide in and out so freaking good.

I shake my head. I can't form a coherent thought. I doubt I can move to do anything.

'You should pull up your shirt and play with your tits.'

I suck in a breath at the suggestion. At the profanity of it. At the dirtiness.

The analytical part of my brain rejects it even as my hands reach for the hem and yank up both layers of material.

The air is hot and sizzles against the taut tips of my nipples. But it's not enough. I need these clothes off. I'm hot, burning up. I want them gone. I wrest them off my head, and Danny smiles at me as he drops his gaze to my chest.

'Oh yeah.' His voice is rough and low as my hands slide onto my breasts. 'That's it. Pinch them. Twist them. I bet you get off on a little pain.'

I mentally reject the notion, but something dark and dormant stirs to life inside me, and my fingers are a slave to its dictates. My nipples are already elongated with arousal, and I pinch the tips and twist them at the same time. A shard of white, hot pain lances through them. The sensation shudders through my body, and I moan.

It hurts so damn good.

'Hell yessss. I felt that all the way down here.' His eyes are darker now, hotter, as his fingers scissor inside me, and I moan. 'Oh yeah... your pussy likes that too, clamping down so fucking tight.'

Danny obviously doesn't believe in using the proper terms for body parts. He lifts his gaze to meet mine. 'You look hot touching yourself, Doc.'

The compliment cascades over me, and I twist my nipples at the same time his fingers thrust inside, and electricity arcs between the two, a white-hot streak of lightning, vicious in its erotic intensity.

He smiles. 'I knew you'd be like this. I knew you'd be hot and tight and wet.' His fingers punctuate each word with a deep thrust. 'I knew your tits would look like this as you gave it up for me.'

His words fill my head with their arrogant certainty. They make me mad as hell and so freaking turned on I can barely breathe.

'I knew you wanted me.' He adds another finger, and my hips rotate as the stretch burns so damn good. 'That you'd spread your legs for me.' He withdraws and slams into me again, and I moan as he sets an insane rhythm, ploughing his clever fingers into me over and over. 'I knew you'd do whatever the hell I wanted when I got you on your back.'

I want to deny it, but he's right – I've known it, too. Known it was only a matter of time before this happened, before I was flat on my back for him. Giving him whatever the hell he wanted. It's why I've been running so damn hard in the other direction.

His mouth, as he speaks, is as mesmerising as his eyes, and I want to kiss it despite his arrogance. I want to feel it against mine. I want his tongue thrusting inside me as deep and sure as his fingers.

'Kiss me.' It comes out on a gasp as he adds another digit, and my hips buck at the invasion. I lift my head, my lips seeking his as my fingers clamp tight around my nipples.

He lowers his mouth so it hovers just over mine. He smells like soap and coffee. He smiles and shakes his head.

'Can't. A deal's a deal, Doc.'

I growl my displeasure as he removes his mouth from my vicinity and I collapse back against the duvet. He laughs, and I hate him some more, but he's relentless then, pulling his fingers out of me, ignoring my moan of protest as they glide to my clitoris, pinching and flicking and rubbing hard, just like I need it, just like I've always needed it.

No guy has ever known that about me. But Danny – a virtual stranger – knows it instantly. Knows that I need relentless pressure on my clitoris – almost brutal. Not soft or slow or gentle but fast and fierce and furious.

The orgasm starts in my toes and spreads north like wildfire, gathering momentum as it rolls through every muscle group and along every nerve ending until I shake with it. But I'm scared to give it free rein. Scared it'll consume me and I'll burn up in this elevator and never know anything like this again and, perversely, I don't want it to keep going because then it will end, and I don't want it to end.

'Let it go, Doc.' His voice is low and rough and urgent as he hangs over me, his eyes boring into mine, hot, insistent. 'Let it go.'

I can't. It's trembling hard through my muscles, but I push it back. I just can't.

His head swoops down then, and he kisses me, licking into my mouth, and the electricity is in his tongue and I break, crying out his name as my body bows off the floor, consumed by the maelstrom.

The blizzard is inside me now, but it's hot, not cold, lashing me with heat and raining me with fire. It buffets my body, and I am lost to its push and pull.

I give in to it. To the fork and sizzle of the lightning, licking hot tongues everywhere. To the deep plunder of his mouth. To the mad pound of my heart. My body is the grateful beneficiary of his experience, and I let him tutor me right to the end.

My orgasm reaches its crescendo, and I cry out as it takes me, my pulse as loud as the blizzard inside my head. Danny's fingers know just what to do to prolong the ecstasy, and I buck against them, wringing out every last second of pleasure, holding on as long as I can.

But then it's over, the storm spirals away, and I'm so excruciatingly sensitive where he's touching me I whimper against his mouth and grab for his wrist, wrenching it out of my pants.

'Stop,' I gasp against his mouth.

I vaguely hear him chuckle, and his smiling face floats above me as he looms there again for a beat or two before he collapses beside me. I know how he feels. I'm like a toasted marshmallow at the moment – a burnt crisp on the outside, a puddle of goo in the middle.

We contemplate the ceiling together. Only the sound of our breathing disturbs the silence. I love that his is as erratic as mine and I listen to it as I slowly recover, my eyes drifting shut.

'You want to talk about the weather now?'

I laugh. It's been my experience that round about this time, a new sexual partner usually asks how it was. Not Danny. He doesn't have to. The man knows I just had the best sexual experience of my life.

And there hadn't even been proper... penetration.

I can barely keep my eyes open now. An intense orgasm on top of zero sleep is a lethal combination. I'm only just conscious of rolling on my side, of snuggling against him, of his warm arm sliding around my shoulders. I think I sigh and I vaguely feel his lips brush the top of my head, but then sleep pulls at my eyelids and I fall headfirst into slumber.

* * *

I don't know how long I sleep for. All I know, as I float up through the layers to consciousness, is I'm cocooned in warmth, and my nose is pushed against a firm cushiony muscle. There is dim light and hard floor beneath me as my eyes flutter open, and I confront a flat, brown nipple.

I'm fully awake now, my body reacting before my brain gets into gear. I glance up into the sleeping face of a very familiar man, his mouth slack, his whiskery jaw so damn tactile. I'm asleep in Danny Colton's arms?

I frantically think back. The blizzard. The heating in my apartment. Knocking on Danny's door. Getting into the elevator with him.

Oh no...

I blink, my head jerks up, flight or fight kicks in, and I choose both as my brain grapples for explanations.

What did I do?

Unfortunately, it all comes back to me – Danny's hand down my pants, Danny talking dirty to me, Danny kissing me, Danny making me come – as I scuttle backwards, crablike. I have to get as far away from him as possible in an elevator that suddenly feels about as large as a postage stamp.

I scuttle until the wall hits my back and then I scuttle up until I'm standing, and I stare at him, horrified for a beat or two, until every detail of what we did comes back, and I drag my eyes off him. I snag my reflection in the dull aluminium finish on the opposite wall.

Good lord!

I stare at the woman who looks back at me, her hair in a cloud around her head and completely naked from the waist up. My pulse splutters in my chest as I look down at myself.

Yep. Topless.

What on earth is the matter with me? I cover my nudity with crossed arms, but I still don't recognise the woman opposite. The woman whose driving force until she got in this elevator was to save as many grandmothers as she could from the results of car wrecks.

'Looking for this?'

Everything inside me freezes at the deep, male voice. My gaze cuts to the floor where Danny is now on his side, propped up on a bent elbow as my shirt dangles from his fingertips. He doesn't bother to suppress his amusement.

Leaning forward with both my hands still crossed in front of me, I snatch it off him and press the scrunched fabric to my chest to cover my modesty. He watches me and my pulse hammers madly as I contemplate how to put on my shirt without flashing at him.

'You need me to fill you in on what happened?'

I shake my head. 'It's all coming back to me.'

He smiles a big smile. 'You're freaking out about it, aren't you?'

I shake my head. I have levels of freaking out at the moment, and level one is my state of dress. Maybe I could ask him to turn around?

'Could you... do you think you could turn around so I can put my shirt on?'

That's how bamboozled I am because I could just turn around, but it doesn't occur to me right at this moment. I'm caught between mortification and some sick kind of wantonness that likes the way he's looking at me with such frank appreciation.

He shakes his head, slow and deliberate. 'Hell, no.'

I didn't expect him to refuse, and my breath catches. But I suddenly have bigger concerns. I finally notice he's not wearing a shirt, either. Acres of tan – despite living in the middle of the Rocky Mountains – and tattoos stretch smooth and taut over flat abs and wide, round shoulders. I blink and drag my eyes off a chest cluttered with ink that I suddenly want to lick.

*Concentrate, Holly.*

He came into this elevator wearing a T-shirt and a hoodie, which are now both on the floor. I sift through my addled brain, trying to remember when it came off, but I can't. I'm sure it was still on when I drifted off to sleep.

'Where's your shirt?'

'I took it off about half an hour ago.' He shrugs. 'It's hot enough in here without having a woman plastered all over you.'

'Oh.' Warmth floods my cheeks, adding to the heat already in abundance. I suck in a breath of stuffy air and send out a quick prayer for imminent rescue.

He looks me over like he's contemplating what to do with me next, and my breath cuts off in my throat; my organs melt down. A voice yammers at the back of my head.

*Put your shirt on, Holly.*

But I'm too caught up in the contemplation of his gaze to listen to it. My legs tremble as his gaze lingers everywhere, and I'm glad for the solid bulk of the wall behind.

'I'm hungry,' he announces.

I blink. With him looking at me like this, food is the last thing on my mind. But his sculpted musculature looks like it needs a lot of calories to keep it pumped and primed. He pushes to a sitting position in one graceful move-ment, and my throat is suddenly dry as toast.

He does that slow prowl towards me again until he's close enough to sit back on his haunches. I should be mortified that he's practically sitting at my feet, his head level with my crotch, his gaze wandering slowly over my body, his nostrils flaring.

But I just feel dizzy. And taut with anticipation.

A man is at my feet, gazing up at me, his focus intense. The hard thump of my heart bounds through my abdomen and pushes against all my pulse points.

'You might have to wait till we get out of here.' I clear my throat, my voice annoyingly raspy.

He shakes his head slowly, his smile growing bigger. 'I have plenty to eat.'

I'm confused for a moment. Then his hand lands on the fabric of my shirt, just under where I clutch it to my chest. He tugs it, and some of it slips through my fingers to reveal the upper swells of my breasts. I grip harder, resisting the pull.

'What are you doing?' My voice, still husky, hovers in the air as heavy as the throb between my legs.

He doesn't take his eyes off me. 'I want to look at you.' His words are like a caress. Like he's leaned forward and brushed his lips against my belly. 'Then I'm going to eat you.'

My stomach clenches tight. The crude statement shocks me so much that when he tugs again, the shirt slips from my hands. I'm laid bare to him now, and his gaze zeroes in on my breasts. My nipples pucker at his intense interest, and he smiles knowingly.

I should be embarrassed at my exposure, but my brain is still stuck back at the eating part. He isn't hungry for food and everything below my belly button clenches.

He wants to... He's going to... go down on me.

Without taking his gaze from the diamond-hard tips of my nipples, his hands slide up the sides of my legs, and my skin tingles in their wake. He's going slowly. I know I can stop him at any moment. I know he will stop if I ask. All I have to do is open my mouth and tell him no. Such a simple two-letter word.

So easy to say.

But my heart is thundering, and my throat is dry, and I'm so drenched between my legs with wanting I can smell it. He can, too, the flare of his nostrils tells me so. And I want this. For him to put his mouth to me.

To... eat me.

I've never achieved orgasm the two other times a guy has gone down on me. Never. But I liked it. I liked it a lot. And everything is hot and tight and tingling, and I'm so primed for another climax that Danny will probably only need to breathe on me down there and I'll come all over his face.

The thought is shocking. And so damn titillating.

For a moment, I wonder if Danny planned this whole thing somehow and he's rigged some kind of aerosolised drug or aphrodisiac to slowly diffuse into the ventilation system of the elevator. Because this isn't like me. I don't do stuff like this.

Until today. Today, suddenly, I crave it.

I push the thought aside. This is Danny. He's not the grand master plan kinda guy. Too elaborate for Mr Laid Back. And why conjure up a blizzard and trap women in elevators when he can just crook his finger? When he can look at me and tell me he can get me off with just one hand and I let him?

Why extend himself?

His fingers reach my waistband, and his gaze seeks mine. 'Whaddya reckon, Doc? Care to help a starving man out?'

The air almost sizzles as my breath huffs out. I don't say yes, exactly, because I'm too enthralled to form coherent words, but when he hooks his thumbs under my waistband, I don't object. I just stare at him, my lips parted, my breathing a series of soft, ragged pants.

His eyes stay locked on mine as he peels three layers of clothing – sweatpants, long johns, underwear – down in one smooth movement. All the way down. His gaze never leaves mine, even as his hands urge me to step out of the confines altogether, including my socks, and he tosses them over his shoulder.

Only when I'm fully naked does he break eye contact, his gaze meandering down, down, down until he reaches the juncture of my thighs, and his breath hisses from his lungs in an audible stream.

'Oh yes,' he whispers.

He stares for a long time, his nostrils flaring, his mouth slightly parted, and my heart beats, and my mouth waters, and the slickness builds between my legs. My rectus abdominis muscles behind my belly button pull tauter and tauter.

I swear I hear them creak under the tension.

He leans forward and brushes his mouth against my inner upper thigh, and a low moan gurgles in the back of my throat. It's loud, though, in the cloistered air of the elevator, louder again as he repeats the caress on the other side. His breath is hot on my leg as he nuzzles closer and closer to where I need him most.

A hand slides onto my right ankle, and I startle at the unexpectedness. My pulse spikes, but he just urges my leg up and over his shoulder, baring me fully to his view. And he looks fully. I'm the most exposed I've ever been to a man's gaze, and I'm so turned on I can barely breathe.

He flicks his gaze up. 'I usually like to take my time when I eat, but I'm in the mood for some fast food right now.' He brings those sexy, wicked lips so close to my own slick, swollen ones, I swear they quiver beneath the fan of his breath. Our gazes mesh. 'You might want to hold on to that railing, Doc.'

He's on me then, his mouth opening over me, and I gasp and writhe as his tongue immediately hits the target, as relentless as his fingers had been. My supporting leg threatens to buckle, and I grab for the railing at the same time his hand grips the thigh to shore me up.

I twist my other hand in his hair as our gazes lock tight, and he watches my face as his tongue flays me relentlessly. He watches the way I gasp and pant and the way my breasts sway and bounce and the way my face moves. The way it twists and contorts with the pleasure ripping right through my middle.

My hips start to rock of their own accord, and my hand flattens against the back of his head, holding him there, right there where his tongue is hitting just the right spot. His hand finds my ass, clamping tight so he can keep hitting the spot, and all the time we stare into each other's eyes, and the look in his steals my breath.

He's loving it. He's loving every second.

Maybe it's that look. Maybe it's his technique. Or maybe it's because I've already come once and my body knows the way. Most likely it's because a guy I barely know except to yell at and hate on is performing cunnilingus on me in a broken-down elevator in the middle of a blizzard.

Whatever it is, it's working. I'm his burger and fries to go. And I'm ready to go.

I break, crying out loud. A powerful contraction slams into me and the blizzard is back. It roars through my pelvis like an electrical current, and I cry out. His hand clamps harder, his tongue works faster. Another follows and another until they're ripping through my body as hot and hard and heavy as the breath sawing in and out of my lungs.

The desire to throw back my head, to arch my back, rides my spine like a demon, but I can't tear my gaze from his. I don't want to look away from him.

Look away from him watching me. Look away from him watching me from between my legs as the orgasm he's giving me owns my ass.

So I don't. I ignore the urge to shut my eyes and stay with him until the very end. Stay with him until the orgasm has faded and his tongue is swiping long and slow against my quivering flesh, and my legs really do give out, and he chuckles softly against my thighs as he eases me down beside him.

# 4

## DANNY

She doesn't go straight to sleep this time, and neither do I. My heart is practically punching out of my chest as we lie on the floor and recoup. I may have been giving, not receiving, but tonguing Holly to orgasm and holding her through it was intense. And the expression on her face as she came – full of the wonder of it – makes me feel like king of the fucking world.

I want to savour it.

The way I'm savouring the sweet, musky taste of her on my lips and the aroma of her arousal, still thick and intoxicating in my nostrils. This woman is like no woman I've ever met. She's barely been civil to me the past few weeks, despite the lust that lurks in her eyes every time we cross paths, and now here she is, naked and sated beside me.

She let me in; she gave herself over to me.

My cock is hard and my balls ache from sexual denial, but my heart is full, and I've never felt so satisfied. I feel like I've been given a gift. I feel like I could deny myself forever if it means I can pleasure Holly Vincent for the rest of my life. I don't even have to think about it to know it'd be worth the agony.

Already I want to touch her again. Go again.

But I can tell from the tension vibrating off her she's not lying there enjoying the buzz. I can practically hear her thinking. I smile at the ceiling. 'Breathe, Doc. Everything's fine.' Everything is more than fine, as far as I'm concerned. It's fucking awesome.

'I'm breathing.'

I laugh at her choked reply. If someone came into her ER with her respiratory state, she'd probably put oxygen on them. I roll my head to the side to inspect her profile. Her gaze is fixed on the ceiling.

'Now you're freaking out, right?'

Her mouth purses, and she doesn't say anything for a beat or two as she slowly fills her lungs and blows the air out in a slow, steady stream.

'Why on earth would I be freaking out?' she says, her breathing obviously not bad enough to inhibit sarcasm. 'I've only let a guy I barely know put his hands down my pants and then let him go down on me.'

I chuckle as her voice goes all high and breathy again. I plan to do a lot more than that, but I wisely keep it to myself. 'I take it this is outside your usual behaviour.'

She rolls her head to fix me with a look, and I like how close our mouths are and the warmth of her shoulder as it presses into mine. I grin as she pulls out that haughty looking-down-the-nose thing she's perfected. I wonder if she knows she does it?

'You take it right.'

'It's okay. Like I say—' My gaze drops to her mouth. A memory of it parted and panting as she came slices straight to my groin. The thought of it wrapped around my cock makes me want to groan out loud. 'What happens in the elevator...'

She blushes and rolls her head back to centre and trains her eyes on the ceiling again, but I'm encouraged by the fact she hasn't tried to cover herself yet.

'It's been fun though, right?'

'That's hardly a reason to do anything.'

I full-out laugh this time. I think fun is the reason to do a lot of things, and I'm hit with the sudden desire to show this woman some fun. She does an important job, pretty much to the exclusion of all else, from what I can see – I wouldn't mind being her fun.

'No offence, Doc,' I tease, 'but a chick who doesn't even masturbate doesn't get to be the fun police.'

The colour in her cheeks goes from pink to crimson. 'I didn't say I didn't.'

'Ahhh. I get it.' I nod and suppress a grin. It's probably wrong I get off on teasing her. It's like verbal foreplay, and my nerves itch with anticipation. My dick twitches. 'It's okay if you use a mechanical device instead, Doc. No shame in it.'

She rolls her head to glare at me. 'I'm not talking with you about... dildos.'

I smile as I roll up on my side and look down at her. She's glorious, all stretched out and naked. In the dim light, her skin glows milky pale, her nipples a light mocha, her dark hair spread out around her head like an ebony halo. 'If I was a patient, you would.'

'You're not.'

'Just say I was?' I persist for no other reason than I like to hear the D word coming from her lips and the way saying it puts colour in her cheeks.

'Believe it or not, most patients don't come into the ER to have a conversation about dildos. Not unless one is irretrievably stuck up their ass.'

I blink, shocked by her matter-of-factness, considering the pinkness in her face. I laugh. 'Seriously?'

'Seriously. We have an ass box full of things that people have shoved up their rectums and need medical assistance to retrieve. Plenty of dildos in there. It kind of puts you off owning one.'

'So you don't own one?'

There was a long pause. 'No.'

'Because of the ass box? I hate to break it to you, Doc, but if you do it right, you should be pretty safe.'

She rolls her eyes at me. 'Look, despite present behaviour to the contrary, I'm just not that... sexually daring.'

I almost laugh. A dildo is sexually daring? But I don't want her to clam up. I want her to keep talking, so I suppress the tickle in my vocal cords.

'And if you think I have even two minutes of my life to spare for sexual recreation, then you're crazy.'

'Thought you docs were always banging in the on-call rooms?'

She half laughs, half snorts. 'Are you kidding? Even if I could find the time and the inclination to commit a potentially career-ending act at work, there's no privacy in those places. No locks, either. This is real life. Not television.'

'In which case, you definitely need a dildo in your life.'

Or a building super on speed dial...

'I'll think about it when I'm thirty-five and I might finally have some spare time to utilise it.'

It is depressing as hell that this highly sexual woman, who has blown apart

in my arms twice this morning, is living an asexual life. Her acceptance of it is
even more so.

'So, the city can thank you for this blizzard,' I say, determined now to cram
our time in the elevator with as much sexual recreation as possible.

And fill every other spare moment of her life with it, too, after we get out of
here – if I play my cards right.

She frowns. 'How do you figure that?'

'Clearly, the universe was trying to get you laid, and even it knew drastic
measures were required.'

She doesn't say anything for a second, then her face smooths out, and she
laughs, her shoulders shaking, her boobs shifting hypnotically with the movement. I don't think I've ever seen her laugh, and it's so fucking sexy I feel it all
the way down to my aching balls.

I kiss her then, I can't help myself. She's irresistible and she opens to me on
a moan and slowly winds her arms around my neck, presses her tits to my
chest, her nipples two hard points, and we're panting and breathing hard
within seconds. My pulse crashes through my head and bounds through the
shaft of my cock, increasing the pain tenfold. I want to rip down my jeans and
plunge inside her.

'Christ,' I mutter against her mouth and pull away before I do rip them
down and fuck her into the floor. My wallet and stash of condoms are in the
apartment, and besides, I want this to be about her.

I roll onto my back. I know she's as turned on as I am; I can hear it in the
husky rasp of her breathing. I know I could roll her under me and have her.
I've always known that. But I resist, mentally quelling the revolt in my testicles.

'You don't want to...?'

Her hesitant question wraps a hand around my heart and squeezes. I like
that she's tentative. A lot of women I've been with would just jump on top –
behaviour I fully endorse – but who knew shyness was this arousing? 'No
condom.'

She's quiet for a moment, then she sits upright. I enjoy the view as everything shifts nicely, before she draws her knees up and covers all the good bits.
Her gaze falls on my crotch, and my dick bucks against the zipper, practically
punching a hole in my jeans. It wants out. The ache in my balls intensifies.

She glances over her shoulder at me. 'I may not be the sexual athlete you
appear to be—'

'Hey,' I protest on a laugh.

She smiles and carries on. 'But even I know there's more than one way to...' I tense, hoping she doesn't say *skin a cat*. My dick is in enough pain. 'Get a guy off. I am a doctor, you know.'

I chuckle and stroke my index finger up her spine, because I can't not touch her. She shivers slightly, and goosebumps fan out from my touch.

'And it's the least I can do, after...'

She lowers her gaze slightly, but she doesn't look away. Or blush or squirm. My body throbs with the urge to sink inside her, but I know a little denial won't kill me.

Christ, I hate denial.

'I don't expect quid pro quo, Doc.' She cocks an eyebrow, and I laugh. 'Yeah, I know some Latin.'

She laughs too. 'Well, you're just full of surprises, aren't you?'

My fingers draw lazy patterns on her back. 'You have no idea.'

Her smile fades a little, and she looks away, resting her chin on her knees. Her hair falls forward, obscuring her from my view, and if I could kick my own ass I would. I've just reminded her how much she doesn't know about me. Reminded her that what she's doing inside this broken-down elevator with me is completely out of character.

I've brought the outside world into our bubble, reminded her there's a world outside these four walls.

Well done, douchebag.

I scramble to drag her back inside the bubble the only way I know how. She wants some sexual adventure, right? 'Maybe I could go in for a little quid pro quo. If you're up for a challenge?'

Her head turns slowly until her amber eyes fix on me. They glitter with sexual interest. Her lips part slightly in the kind of pout that betrays her arousal. 'What did you have in mind?'

'Do you think you could get me off with just your hand down my pants? No taking my jeans off, no kissing, no touching other than your hand wrapped around my cock.'

Her nostrils flare when I say *cock*. I like it. I also like how fully she looks at me now, like she's decided to throw caution and shyness to the wind.

'I mean, it is in pain, and—' I smile. 'You are a doctor, right?'

She purses her lips as her gaze drops to my crotch before returning to my face, her expression serious. Christ, her doctor face is a turn-on, too. 'I'm not sure... tugging on it's going to help with the pain.'

'Oh it will, Doc, trust me.'

She smiles now. 'I could... examine it for you?'

Her banter is like fingernails stroking my balls. 'I like the way you think.'

'I'll be gentle.' My hand slips from her back as she shifts suddenly. 'I promise.'

My breath catches as she twists and throws her leg over my lap, straddling my upper thighs. She's glorious, her tits high and firm, her nipples mocha-lite, her shoulders back, her hair falling over them like a swathe of dark silk.

Fuck, I'm a dead man.

I slip my hands onto her naked ass. 'No need for gentle. It's kinda robust.'

She slides her hands over mine, which thrusts her tits out perfectly, and I want to curl up and suck each one into my mouth, but she removes my hands from her butt and places them palm down on the floor beside me.

She smiles like suddenly she's found her inner dominatrix and says, 'How about you let the doctor be the judge of that?'

Her fingers grasp the button above my fly and pop it – efficient and detached. They reach for the zip next, brushing against my cock, which bucks at the stimulus. If it's deliberate, she doesn't indicate, and the tension in my dick reaches screaming point.

My zip comes down.

There's no tease, no seduction in her movements; it's methodical, as if I'm just another patient and this is just another examination. But her thighs are straddling me, and she's naked, and her tits are swaying, and I can hear the roughness of her breathing.

Christ, I could come from that clinical look in her eyes alone. And when she reaches inside my underwear and pulls out my cock, I seriously almost do. Everything from my inner thighs to my buttocks to my belly button clenches tight.

'Oh yes.' She stares at it, eyes wide, a dull flush to her cheeks. Her mouth parts temptingly. Her gaze flicks up and meshes with mine. 'That does look painful.'

I lever myself up onto my bent elbows so I can look down at myself. My breath is so hot and thick in my throat it's almost choking me. My fly gapes wide and my cock rises hard and thick and long from the middle. Her hand looks good around my girth and she grips it just right, too – firm and sure.

'What do you suggest, Doc?'

'Well... I'm a big believer in the power of massage.'

Jesus. My heart is beating like a gong against my ribs, and I swallow. 'Me too.'

'It's important to rub lightly, though. To start with.'

Her gaze drifts back to where she holds me, and her hand performs a slow slide down, then an equally slow one all the way up. I groan, and it's so deep and low I swear it comes all the way from my toes. She stops, her hand poised back where it started as she glances at me.

'Too hard?' She smiles an innocent smile. 'Should I stop? I could prescribe rest, maybe?'

I give a half laugh, the muscles that funnel to my cock so tight they'd need a diamond-tipped saw to cut through them. 'Only if you want to see a grown man cry.'

Or beg, for that matter.

She laughs too, her eyes glittering down at me as she tosses her head with the confidence of a woman who has a man by the balls. Her hair swishes around her head and settles on the slopes of her tits. My mouth waters as I think about sucking on those sweet, flushed tips. About pushing them together and thrusting my cock through them, watching my come splatter all over them, massaging it in, tasting its musky flavour on those taut buds.

'I could go a little faster. If you think you can handle it?'

A strangled kind of noise comes from somewhere at the back of my throat as she slides her hand up and down my dick again. My fingers dig into the duvet beside me. 'I can handle it.'

Christ, I'll fucking die if she doesn't.

She does. Her hand picks up the pace, not just moving, but squeezing as well, her thumb swiping over the head of my cock as it nears the top. Her gaze drops to what she's doing, and I almost groan out loud again as her pink tongue wets her bottom lip.

I don't think she's aware she's done it, but fuck, I've been hard for her from the moment I saw her and pretty much most of the last two hours, and she's so beautiful straddling me, her legs wide, the lips of her pussy brushing against the denim of my jeans as she pumps my cock.

Her tits rock with the movement, and her hair brushes her shoulders, and I am dangerously close to the edge. Already the nerves deep inside my butt cheeks are sparking, and there's a pulsing around the base of my spine. It's an exercise in control not to touch her. Not to mash my lips into hers, not to take a nipple in my mouth, not to drag her right on top of my dick and grind.

She flicks a glance at me and finds me watching her. I can't tear my eyes off her. 'It's quite tense still.'

I choke out a half laugh as the pulsing intensifies, and my breath chugs in and out of my chest. 'Not for much longer.'

She drops her gaze briefly to her hand before returning to me.

'It seems to be leaking.' She's all round-eyed and innocent, but she's not fooling me for a second – she's teasing and I fucking love it.

I grin despite the pressure spiking in my balls. 'Keep doing that and it'll do more than leak. It'll start to spit.' I curl up then, I can't help myself – that sassy mouth of hers is like a candy apple, and I want to bite into it.

But she shakes her head, places a stilling hand on my pec. 'A deal's a deal, Danny.'

I groan and drop to my elbows again, my head falling back between my shoulder blades. I should have known that was going to come back and bite me in the ass.

'I think it can take a more vigorous technique now, don't you think?'

My permission is clearly not required. By the time I've lifted my head, her hand is a blur on me and sensation floods my body. Her gaze is glued to my cock, her total concentration dizzying. The head is all purple and engorged, and when she slides her other hand inside my jeans to cup my balls, I'm lost.

She squeezes them.

'Fuck.' I grunt as her hot hand clamps tight around them, torturous and goddamn miraculous all at once. A hot ripple contracts my ass as she rolls them and works my cock with her fingers like they were made especially for me – my own personal handmaiden – and it's more than I can stand.

The climax hits me like a cattle prod shoved right at the root of my dick. My hips jerk and I cry out, but it's cut off in my throat as the muscles in my balls and thighs and ass seize up and everything stops. My pulse, my breathing, even my sight, as everything goes a blinding white.

'Yesss.'

I vaguely hear her triumphant whisper, her hand a fury against me now, as the wave of paralysis releases me from its grip and everything returns. The clatter of my heart, the saw of my breathing, and a rainbow of colour as pleasure rips through me, turning me around, turning me upside down, turning me inside out.

'Yes, yes, yes.'

Her voice is raspy, and her eyes are wide as she watches the first jet of come shoot from my cock and splatter on my belly. More follow, and she tracks them too, until my balls have nothing left to give, until the final ripple of my orgasm recedes, and I collapse against the duvet, my elbows no longer able to keep me upright, my heart pounding.

But she's not done with me yet, and I rouse a little as her fingers release their death grip from my cock and start to wander, sliding through my come. I raise my head to watch her as she finger-paints with my spunk, swirling it around, pushing it over my stomach and ribs and higher.

Just as I had fantasised about doing to her.

Surprisingly, it's a turn-on watching her do it to me, too. Watching her getting off on it. And she is. Her nipples are as hard as bullets, and she's rocking on me a little, her pussy lips rubbing against the denim of my jeans as she bites on her bottom lip.

'Having fun there?'

She doesn't look at me. It's as if she's mesmerised by the patterns she's drawing. 'It's important to complete the treatment,' she says, her voice high yet husky, and I wonder if she's even aware of the increasing grind of her pussy on my thigh.

I tuck both hands under my head and settle in for the show. 'You're the doctor.'

The pads of her fingers, wet with my come, push hard against my nipples. It feels fucking incredible, and my dick, previously spent, twitches. 'Put some on yours,' I say, my voice almost a growl at the thought of it. I tense my thigh and push it up hard against her pussy, and she sucks in a breath.

Her glittering eyes meet mine, and she moans, rocking her hips a little faster. She shakes her hair back, her tits thrusting, and she doesn't look like the prim and capable young doctor too tired and busy for life any more. She's just a woman.

A sexy, wanton woman.

Hell, she looks like every supermodel I used to fantasise about fucking when I was fifteen, all rolled into one. The fact she doesn't even know how breathtaking she is right now only makes her hotter.

Her tits rock to the rhythm of her hips, and her mouth is slightly parted as she slides her index fingers through a puddle of spunk. She lifts her hands to her tits and paints her impossibly erect nipples with my come, drawing in a ragged breath, obviously aroused by her own touch. They shine with moisture even in the low light of the elevator, and the feral beast inside my head growls *mine*.

There's no way I can just watch any longer. I want to taste my come on her tits, lick it all off, and I want her to come while I'm doing it. I lift up, grabbing her hands off my chest and pushing them down, sliding her fingers between her legs, keeping my hands on top.

'Make yourself come.'

It's not a suggestion, not a request. It's a command. She's desperate for another orgasm and close, too, if I'm not very much mistaken. I want her to get herself off while I suck her titties. I want to listen to it; I want to hold her through it.

I grunt as her hand obeys, her fingers knocking against mine as they rub frantically between her legs.

Oh, fuck yes.

I leave her to it, my mouth already salivating for a taste of her as it zeroes in on the nearest nipple, thrust right in front of my face, begging for tongue. My hands push her tits together and hold them that way as I suck a hard nub into my mouth. She gasps and arches her back, one hand sliding onto my shoulder for purchase as the other works her clit. Her moans and the taste and smell of me on her fill my head and shoot like an arrow straight to my groin, setting it on fire.

My cock is hard for her again, stiff against my belly, as I devour her tits, switching from one to the other, sucking hard, scraping my teeth against the tips before soothing them with my tongue and starting all over again. Her hips are rocking like crazy now, her hand a blur, the denim practically on fire from the friction.

I don't have to look to know there's a wet patch on my jeans – I can smell how wet she is, how close she is as her hand slides down my back and anchors mid-way, pulling me closer.

'Danny.'

'Yeah, Doc,' I murmur around a mouthful of nipple, my heart beating like a drum through my ears. 'Come for me, baby. Get yourself off.'

She gasps and cries out then, throwing her head back, smooshing her titties into my face, almost suffocating me. I take my punishment like a man, taking full advantage, lashing her stiff nipples with my tongue as her body jerks and convulses on my leg, and she gasps and grinds her way right to the end of her orgasm.

She falls into me as it spirals away, and we collapse against the floor in a tangled heap, and there's nothing but hard breathing between us for long, long moments.

'Well...' she says after a while, when she can talk again, 'in my medical opinion, that treatment seemed to work.' Her lips brush my shoulder. 'It's probably going to be a recurring condition, however.'

I laugh as a warm buzz hums through my body, making me forget about my throbbing cock, the hard floor against my shoulder blades, and the blizzard raging outside. And the fact Holly and I aren't in a relationship.

'Will you be available for future treatment?'

I'm too blissed out to realise I've referred to life outside the elevator again. Thankfully, so is she. 'No need,' she murmurs in a sleepy voice. 'I'm pretty sure you know how to self-administer.'

I smile. I'd rather have my own personal physician. But the thought is lost in the growing heaviness of my limbs and eyelids, despite the state of my dick. It wouldn't be the first time I'd gone to sleep with a woody. I'm only vaguely coordinated enough to grab my T-shirt and make some attempt to wipe the remaining come off my chest before I, too, drift to sleep.

# 5

## HOLLY

The warm body beside me moves, and I wake to a ringing phone. A panelled ceiling and dim lighting remind me instantly where I am. I hear Danny's low voice as he picks up the phone. I listen to the one-sided conversation, because it's preferable to thinking about what I've done with him and wondering how on earth I'm ever going to go back to my old life after such a... climactic day.

'She thinks they'll be another hour,' he says as he hangs up the phone. His face looms from on high as he looks down, a smile warming his sexy face. My gaze drifts up his legs – they're very long from this vantage point. He's tucked himself away at some stage but the button above his zipper has been left temptingly open.

'Hey, sleepy head.' My heart does a funny little jiggle at his smile and the very familiar way his gaze runs over my body.

An hour. One more hour of being Elevator Holly. It stretches in front of me with possibilities but perversely doesn't seem long enough.

'Are you hungry?'

I'm pretty sure he's actually talking about food this time. So the answer would be no. Not hungry. For food, anyway. I'm hungry for more of him. For more of us. Even the thought of him and me being an us is preposterous. I don't have time for an us. Being an us with anyone is not part of my short-term plan.

But I'm lying here naked in front of him – in front of Danny the building manager – and nothing else matters but touching him. Him touching me.

I'm scarily obsessed.

'A little, sure.' I lie because the last thing he wants is to hear that crazy kind of talk from me. He's made the best of a crappy situation here, of which I am the grateful recipient. The last thing he needs is for accommodating elevator chick going all bunny boiler on him.

'But I can wait an hour.'

'Not me.' He grins. 'I've worked up a real appetite. And I wouldn't be surprised if Bob has a little something in his bag.'

He shuffles off to the bag, which was discarded in the corner when the elevator first shuddered to a halt. In all the… activity, I'd forgotten about its existence. I watch as he sits his ass down next to it and hauls it into his lap. The muscles in his arms move nicely under the caramel tone of his skin.

He really is a pleasure to watch.

'It's like the fucking Tardis in here.' His head is practically in the bag as he hunts around, the shaggy fall of his hair obscuring his face from me. It doesn't matter. Those cheekbones and the deep groves of his dimples are burned into my retinas. I'll never forget his face, not as long as I live.

'There's everything in here, bar the kitchen sink,' he mutters as he starts to pull things out. 'There has to be food.'

I'll never forget making him come, either. His cock – the way he casually uses that term melts me on the inside – is beautiful. It's hard to be impressed by genitals when I see so many of them in my day-to-day job – in all their variations.

The good, the bad, and the downright ugly.

I've become desensitised to them. For me, they're functional. Anatomical. And, frankly, unattractive. But Danny's… I shiver thinking about it.

It's beautiful.

Long and thick in my hand, the petal-soft skin stretched tight over a shaft of forged steel, the veins a work of art. It had taken all my willpower not to wrap my lips around it.

My mouth waters and my nipples tighten just thinking about how he might taste. About whether I could take him all the way to the back of my throat. About what technique he prefers when a woman goes down on him.

My gut burns at the thought that there will be more women after today.

After me. I hate all of them and suddenly want to keep him trapped in here with me.

Bunny boiler alert!

'Doc.' His voice is a low rumble and my pulse spikes. 'Stop looking at me like that.'

His hot gaze sweeps over me like the beam of a flashlight. It treks back to linger on my aroused nipples. The sudden tension in his frame, like he might pounce on me any second, stirs my belly, and it quivers at the flare of heat in his eyes. My breath is thick in my throat, and I don't know enough about guys like Danny to play games, but Elevator Holly is keen to push some boundaries.

Or jealous enough to, anyway.

'Like what?' I ask breathily.

'Like you're trying to figure out how I like my cock sucked.'

His words slice straight to the slickness between my legs, and heat floods my face. The man may not have X-ray vision, but he can obviously read minds. He grins, knowing he's hit the nail on the head.

'It's very distracting,' he says as he returns to his search while my heart rate rattles away. 'And I need some sustenance before we go again.'

Muscles deep inside clench at the thought there's more to come, and a host of possibilities flood my mind, but suddenly he pulls something from the bag with an 'Aha!'

'What is it?'

'It's a Hershey's bar. It looks older than God, but who ever heard of chocolate going bad, right?'

I laugh as he rips the packet open and snaps the bar in two. He's obviously never been in an ER. 'For you,' he offers.

The thought of old chocolate doesn't appeal. Not when I have three packets of brand-new Hershey's almond Kisses in the apartment; and besides, I'd rather watch him eat. 'I couldn't possibly deprive you of the sustenance.'

He grins. 'We still have an hour. You're going to need it as much as me.' My clitoris pulses at the promise in his voice, but I shake my head as he waggles it at me. He shrugs and eats the half he offered me in three bites.

He takes his time with the second half. His head rests back against the wall as he slowly savours each square, his gaze savouring my body at the same time. It drifts up and down me and lingers in all the good places. It throbs between my thighs, and my nipples tingle and harden beneath his rapt attention.

Suddenly self-conscious, I look around for my shirt. It's near his thigh. I could probably just reach over and pluck it up, but my bones are dissolving. 'Throw me my shirt.'

'Nope.' He shakes his head, a small smile playing on his mouth. 'I like looking at you naked.'

My breath hitches at his frankness, but I am acutely aware of my nudity now, and I draw the leg closest to him into a bend in an attempt to lessen my exposure. The slick, swollen flesh between my legs quivers deliciously at the action.

'Don't.' His voice is soft but steely, and my thigh trembles. 'I like looking at your pussy best of all.'

My thigh trembles some more at his choice of words and how he says that word in particular. It shouldn't turn me on, but it does, and I blush. God... part of me wants to pull the duvet over me. Part of me wants to spread my legs so he can look his fill.

Who even am I?

The thought makes me jittery, and confusion makes me disagreeable. 'You think I should just lay here buck naked and let you inspect me while you're in a pair of jeans?'

He grins in such a knowing way. 'Uh huh.' And he slips the last square of chocolate into his mouth.

I hate that he's right, but in a few short hours he's made a total wanton of me. My leg, also going the full wanton, slowly slides to the ground again, and his gaze immediately homes in on my... pussy.

His nostrils flare as he lifts his head from the wall to look closer. 'Pretty,' he murmurs.

My breathing is so rough it feels like sand in the back of my throat. 'The least you can do is even up the playing field.'

His gaze returns to my face as he shakes his head. 'No way, Doc. I want to be inside you too fucking much to take my jeans off without a condom in sight.'

I am both crushingly disappointed and incredibly empowered by his admission of barely restrained desire. The thought undulates through my belly, and I arch a little and squirm to relieve the sudden contraction. A low kind of whimper slips from my lips, and he sucks in a breath.

'You want it too, don't you?'

I want him inside me more than I've ever wanted anything. I nod my head, surprisingly not embarrassed to admit my need is as desperate as his.

'You want me to fuck you?'

I exhale a shaky breath. 'Yes.'

'You want to feel my cock sliding into you?' His voice is as husky as mine.

God, yes. I want him filling me up. 'Yes.' I press my thighs together as his words stroke like fingers against my clitoris.

'Fuck.' Danny groans as his head thunks back against the wall. He regards me with half-closed lids, as if he's trying to figure out how he can make it work. He glances down into Bob's tool bag. 'There's not a condom in there. Trust me, I looked. Although there are plenty of dick substitutes. Who needs sex shops when you have a tool bag?'

My breath catches at the thought of Danny pulling out some kind of phallic tool and using it on me. My eyes widen at such a shocking thought, and I press my thighs together harder as I scrub it from my mind.

But Danny has already heard that catch. How could he not? It's silent in the elevator, apart from the odd creak and our heavy breathing. His gaze zeroes in on mine like a heatseeking missile, suddenly intense. Did it get stuffier in here all of a sudden, or has my breathing become so syrupy it's clogging my airways?

He raises his eyebrow slightly. 'Ahhh...'

He drops his gaze to the pile of items he pulled from Bob's bag earlier. His fingers search through it and I follow the action. 'There is this.'

My heart trips in my chest as Danny holds up a screwdriver, still in its packaging. It has a large, black, bulbous handle, decorated with long grooves – for better grip, I suppose. It's not as big or thick as what Danny's packing in those jeans, but it's a close second.

The sound of plastic tearing streaks through my abdomen like a bolt of lightning, and my eyes are drawn to the tool Danny is holding in his hands. He grips it around the shiny, metallic shaft, but it's the handle that has his attention.

And mine.

'Ridged for her pleasure.' He smiles as he lets it fall into the palm of his opposite hand. I can tell from the dull thud it has some weight to it, and things get a little wetter between my legs.

'So, Doc.' His gaze returns to mine. 'Can you handle a screwdriver?'

My words from earlier – dear God, was it only a few hours ago? – come back to haunt me. 'I—' Whatever I'm about to say gets stuck in my throat. I'm torn between rejection of such an act and utter fascination.

'Want me to show you what you've been missing out on in the dildo department?' *Thud.* 'Think of it as a try-before-you-buy experience.' *Thud.* 'I'll be gentle. I promise.' He mimics my words again as the thudding of the handle mimics my heartbeat.

How can I be so appalled and yet so freaking turned on by what Danny's proposing? I've never done anything so outrageous. I work in an ER. How many cases of sexual misadventure have I doctored to?

'Come on, Holly.' His voice is a virtual whisper now. 'Live a little. Say yes.'

My name on his lips shivers down my spine, and it sounds so damn good, I'd grant him just about anything in this moment. Just about. 'And risk ending up in my own emergency department with a screwdriver stuck up my vagina?' I'd never live that down. 'Pass.'

But I am seriously tempted.

'Okay.' He chuckles, low and slow, clearly amused by the prospect. 'As you wish.'

I'm simultaneously relieved and disappointed that he's not going to push a little, but not for long as he displaces the tool bag from his lap and once again prowls towards me, still in possession of the screwdriver. He is panther-like, his tattoos swaying and dancing seductively as his muscles move beneath his flesh.

He stops as he draws close and I'm surprised the entire elevator isn't vibrating to the pound of my heart as he unfurls himself from all fours to settle on his side next to me.

Danny's body presses along the length of mine as he props his head up with one hand and holds the screwdriver in the other, his gaze fanning over my face. 'You're beautiful,' he whispers, and even though I've never felt beautiful thanks to my cosmetic-surgeon-in-the-making ex – who delighted in pointing out how he'd be able to correct all my flaws once he was qualified – the way he's looking at me right now, I feel it.

He makes me feel it.

'Do you trust me?'

Is it strange to admit I do? This guy I barely knew a few hours ago? Who is holding a rather large implement he's just suggested he could use on my body? In my body. As a sex aid. For sexual pleasure. And not just mine.

It's bizarre, but I do trust him. I would never have let him do what he's already done if I didn't.

'Yes.'

He nods like it's a given, but his gaze locks on mine, and it's warm and blue and sincere, and I feel immersed in trust. Slowly, he lowers the handle of the screwdriver to my chest. I gasp as it lands, soft but solid, against my sternum. My breathing cuts out, my nipples peak. My heart kicks so hard, I'm amazed the tool isn't bouncing to the frantic rhythm.

'Shut your eyes,' Danny whispers as he lowers his head to nuzzle just under my ear. 'Keep them shut.'

It might be whispered but it's a command and I swallow, both at the prickle of his whiskers and the anticipation of what he's going to do next as I shut my eyes and give myself over to just feeling. The handle inches across my décolletage to my left breast, nudging the painfully erect nipple before it rolls over the top of it, flattening the hard nub.

Back and forth. Back and forth.

I gasp at the unfamiliar sensation, arching my back. It hurts a little but my whole body lights up. He reverses the process, the handle moving to the other nipple. The erotic press combines with the buzz of anticipation, and I whimper out loud.

'Easy, Doc.'

His voice is a low rumble. His breath fans warm on my skin. Goosebumps prickle my scalp and down the side of my neck.

'I wish this was my cock,' he murmurs, 'all stiff and leaking over your titties.'

My pelvic floor contracts at the wild images exploding in my head. Danny's beautiful cock, thick and hard, the plump head smoothing over my nipples, leaving smears of pre-cum.

'Rubbing all over you.'

The rasp in Danny's breathing is a hot flurry against my skin as he releases his hold on the handle. He reaches for my hand that is squished between us, guiding it, pushing it inside his jeans. His erection brushes my knuckles and I moan, fighting against the urge to open my eyes as his hand departs and my fingers automatically curl around him and squeeze.

'Fuuuck.'

He breathes the profanity into my ear so low and dirty I press my legs together to stop a ripple of sensation becoming something so much more.

Seconds later, the screwdriver is moving again, moving lower, bisecting my abdomen, but in my mind's eye it's no longer a lifeless tool, it's the magnificent structure of steely flesh and bulging veins I now hold in my hand. The slow trajectory south halts at my belly button as Danny dallies there, the touch featherlight now as it circles around and around. I squirm at the stimulus that spreads tentacles of heat right between my legs.

'Mmm,' he mutters, his lips brushing my earlobe. 'My balls feel so good rubbing against you right there, don't they?'

A picture of Danny rotating his hips, the swing of his testicles circling my belly button, jolts right through my core and I swear I can feel the bounce of my abdominal aorta pulsing just below the slow maddening onslaught.

'So... good,' I say on a pant, coherency hard to find in a brain that's dissolving as quickly as my body.

Finally, he drags the screwdriver lower and everything clenches tight in my pelvis as I picture his erection gliding lower and lower. My hand grips the duvet as my fevered imagination anticipates where it'll stop. Will he refrain from going all the way as I've asked?

Do I want him to?

Because right now with my hand down his pants and a porn reel running on the dark screen behind my closed eyes, it's as real as the flesh and blood I'm holding in my hand.

A soft crinkle interrupts the ragged pant of my breath as the touch slides through the light sprinkling of hair covering my mons before Danny finds the slick groove between my labia and nestles there, right over my clitoris. I gasp softly as it contracts almost painfully, like it's been hit with a spark of electricity.

The pressure increases, and I moan, squeezing everything tight inside me. Squeezing him tight in my hand, causing a low rumble in his throat. The noise hums through me, cranking my arousal higher. I'm so turned on, so close to the edge now, I'm petrified it'll all be over before the main act.

'Spread 'em, Doc. My cock needs some room to move.'

I'm so caught up in the anticipation and sensations, I haven't even realised my thighs are still squeezed together. I hesitate a little because I'm turned on AF and I want... I don't know what I want. And that's... scary.

'It's okay,' he murmurs, his voice soft and patient. 'I promise.'

The sincerity of his tone reassures me as I ease my trembling, jellified legs apart. I'm so slippery now the screwdriver slides down of its own accord. I feel it pressing against my entrance, thick and blunt like the head of his cock, and I squeeze his erection as if it's what is nestled between my legs right now.

'Jesus, Holly.' The way he breathes my name like that, like a benediction, kicks my arousal up another level. 'You're so fucking wet.'

I pant as I run my thumb over his leaking tip. 'You are too,' I say, my voice so husky I barely recognise it as mine.

'I'm about to get wetter,' he says, and then his lips brush my ear as he whispers, 'You ready to use that big brain of yours?'

I nod at his hoarse enquiry because speaking seems impossible now.

'Good,' he mutters. 'I'm thrusting inside you now. Can you feel me?'

There's nothing but some increased pressure from the outside, but in my imagination I feel the thick hard push of him in every cell of my body as he enters me. I gasp as lights flare behind my eyes. 'Yes,' I say on a moan, my hand squeezing him rhythmically now.

He groans. 'Oh Holly, baby, you feel so fucking tight.'

'More.'

'You want more?' he pants into my ear.

'Yes.'

'You want me to fuck you harder?'

I cry out at the thought and squeeze him harder. 'Yes.'

'How's that?' He grunts once, twice, three times as if he's thrusting. 'Fucking you into the floor. Can you feel it?'

My response isn't decipherable, coming from somewhere in the back of my throat because even though I'm totally in my head now, picking up the fantasy he's putting down, I feel every moment, every sensation. His big body is hunched over mine, his hips are a piston splitting me in two as he slams in and out, in and out, in and out.

'God, Holly.' He groans and presses a row of kisses down my neck. 'You should see your face.'

A part of me wants to open my eyes to see his face, but the fact Danny is watching me as he narrates this dirty-talking fantasy increases my arousal tenfold. If I open my eyes, reality might intrude – the real Holly might appear. And I like this Holly, even if I don't recognise her.

'In and out,' he says, continuing his low, rough narration, and I almost come from that alone. I swear I feel the first low pulse deep, deep inside. 'In and out.'

The pressure eases externally but I barely register it as behind my lids, Danny fucks me into the floor. I barely register his hand sliding up to the hard, engorged knot of nerves between my legs. I'm so sensitive there I cry out as he presses his fingers against it.

'Shhh,' he whispers, 'you're okay, I got you.'

I don't have to see to know his mouth is hovering over mine. His warm breath bathes my lips and my tongue flicks out to wet them from the dry rasp of my panting.

'That's right,' he says as his fingers circle. 'In and out. Think about my cock pounding in and out. Because it's always going to be my cock that you fantasise about from now on, isn't it, Holly?'

'Yes.' My clitoris pulses as my core pulls tight. Danny has ruined me for other men.

'When you're touching yourself late at night,' he persists, warm air puffing against my mouth as fantasy Danny's cock fills and stretches me.

'Yes.'

'Good,' he mutters, increasing the tempo of his fingers.

There's something about Danny's fingers that are perfect for the job. Rough to my smooth, thick to my slender, finessed to my fumbling. And so damn knowing, working my clitoris like he must work his drumsticks, deft and sure.

He kisses me then and I moan, the taste of chocolate teasing me. I squeeze his cock and lick into his mouth, needing more – deeper and harder like his fantasy thrusts that feel so startlingly real. His groan fills my head and when he says, 'I'm right to the hilt, Holly, come for me now,' against my mouth – I am gone.

My body flares in one bright, blinding flash. I gasp, breaking our lip-lock at the sudden, violent clench of my walls around the imagined unyielding thickness of his cock high and hard inside me. Pleasure bursts like popping candy from deep inside my pelvis and I cry out as my body shudders through a pleasure so violent I'm not sure I'll survive it.

'Jesus, Doc, you're hot when you come,' Danny whispers in my ear as I thrash and gasp. 'I can't decide what I want more right now. To fuck you or to eat you.'

His words push me higher, and I hold on for as long as I can, clinging to Danny and the pleasure until it starts to tail away, and I'm left panting and limp in its wake.

When I'm finally quiet, he eases my hand out of his underwear and gathers me close. He's still hard and I think maybe I should do something about that, but my brain is mush as he kisses my forehead and we just lie there in the aftermath. For a minute or two anyway, until I hear clanging and banging and voices.

'That'll be the cavalry,' he announces.

And in an instant, everything changes.

* * *

Twenty minutes later, we're free and our rescuers have departed, leaving us alone again. I don't know what to say now as I try not to be the person I was before getting in the elevator and having my world rocked. I guess I knew there'd be a reckoning, but I didn't count on it being this brutal.

What the hell had I been thinking?

'Why don't you come back to my place?' he suggests. 'The blizzard's still raging out there.'

It's a tantalising idea, and I allow myself the luxury of it for a beat or two before I pull myself back from the edge. 'I need to sleep. I have to study later.'

He shrugs. 'You can study at my place.'

I almost laugh out loud at that. If I go to his place, we're both going to be naked in seconds. I'm pretty sure my clothes are going to fall off every time I see him from now on.

Best to just not see him.

What happened in the elevator was amazing, but I can't afford the luxury of long days and nights in bed with Danny. I don't have enough spare time for me, let alone him.

'Look... it was nice, but...'

He winces. 'Nice?'

I think about the screwdriver. Yeah, okay. It was a lot of things – nice wasn't one of them. 'I'm sorry, I just don't have time in my life for—'

'Dalliances.'

I half-smile. 'Right.'

'We'll see.' He smiles that irritatingly cocky smile, and I remember why I've kept my distance all this time.

'What's that supposed to mean?'

'It means I think you're going to miss me.'

Okay, so we're back to words of one syllable again. 'You're not part of my plan, Danny.'

'And that's what? Become an ER hotshot, marry a surgeon, live in the burbs in a fancy house, two point four kids? No screwing building supers?'

My entire body rejects this picture of dull domestic suburbia. He has no idea what I want from my life. Nor am I about to tell him. Danny's time is up and that's that. 'At the moment, I'll settle for passing my residency.'

He smiles and he's that laid-back guy again. 'Fair enough. Go to bed. I'll fix your heating.'

'Thank you. Be careful on the stairs,' I add, because I don't want him breaking his neck.

'I will. And you know where I am if you need more of what I can give you.'

I grit my teeth at his arrogance at the same time my toes curl in my Uggs. 'I won't.'

He just raises an eyebrow and turns away, completely unperturbed by my denial. His ass draws my gaze because I'm only human. Heat floods my face as I spy the screwdriver shoved in his back pocket. It's morbidly fascinating, and I can't unglue my gaze from it.

He looks over his shoulder at me and grins, his dimples flashing. Like he knew I was going to be staring after him.

Like he knows I'll be knocking on his door for more of what he can give me.

I harden my resolve not to. And throw up a little prayer for strength. *No screwing building supers, Holly.*

*Get a grip.*

# 6

## DANNY

My forearm throbs under the temporary bandage I've wrapped around it. Not as much as my dick throbs, though, as I cross the parking lot to the hospital's ER. It's been bitching at me for the past week – since the elevator – and now it's happy as a fucking clam.

No. I didn't deliberately cut myself just for an excuse to see Holly again. I can walk up a flight of steps and do that if I want. But I was thinking about her as I picked up the shards of glass off the floor behind the bar, instead of concentrating on what I was doing, and fell into the middle of the mess when someone from behind gave me an accidental nudge.

So I don't have anyone else to blame.

It's actually not that bad, despite the bar owner's cold sweat over a potential lawsuit. It could probably do with a few stitches, but I've had worse. Normally, I wouldn't bother anyone with it – just tape it up and leave it for a few days. But the universe just handed me a perfect excuse to bother Holly, and I take it with both hands, even if it is two in the morning.

It's a relief to finally walk inside the hospital. The blizzard may have blown itself out days ago, but it's still as cold as fuck. I haven't missed the winters here, how the air stabs like icicles in my lungs. A blast of heat at the entrance doors welcomes me, and I unzip my parka with my good hand.

I follow the signs for triage, the antiseptic smell of the place enveloping me.

It seems quiet to my untrained eye. It's early hours of the morning, I suppose, but I figure the time of day doesn't matter a whole lot in an ER.

I come to a desk, and there's an efficient-looking black woman, mid-thirties, at a computer in a pair of scrubs. Her name tag tells me she's Trisha. I smile at her, which is usually guaranteed to melt most women – Holly being the exception. This woman too, apparently, as she looks me up and down, obviously not impressed.

'How can I help?'

I know instinctively that if I present my arm I'll probably spend half the night in the chairs, so I keep my injury below the raised ledge of the desk. 'I'd like to see Dr Vincent.'

I know she's working tonight. She left just before me in her regular work clothes, her stethoscope hanging from her fingers.

'And who might you be?'

'Danny. Colton. I'm a neighbour. She'll want to see me.' That's a lie. I have no idea whether she'll see me or not, but I'm hoping she will. I hope she considers the hospital neutral ground for us. I hope she's as desperate as I am for more than a glimpse.

'Why don't we let Dr Vincent be the judge of that?' Trisha picks up a phone, her eyes firmly trained on me. 'There's a guy called Danny Colton, says he's your neighbour, asking for you.'

The woman nods twice, then puts the phone back on the cradle. She tips her chin in the direction of some doors and says, 'Go through.'

I smile at Trisha, who ignores me, but I barely register the snub as I start towards the doors. I push them as I get near enough, and they open into a large space with a central workstation lapped by a bunch of mostly empty gurneys parked in bays around the perimeter of the room. The lights are dim, and there's not a lot of bustle going on here.

'Danny?'

I turn to find Holly coming at me from a dark corridor. She's in scrubs, her hair is pulled back in a low ponytail, and her stethoscope, which is slung around her neck now, swings a little against her tits as she strides closer.

It's hot as fuck. She's hot as fuck, all capable and confident.

In the elevator, she'd been in my domain, totally out of her depth. Here, the shoe is on the other foot. She's the one in charge, she's the boss, and my cock roars to life again. Not even her frowny face has an effect. She's obviously annoyed at my presence, but goddamn if that's not a turn on too.

She's the perfect woman right now – sexy, pissed off, powerful. And I want inside those scrubs so fucking hard.

'What do you want?' she demands, her voice low and short, as she crosses her arms. 'I have paperwork up to my eyeballs.'

'Well, see...' I lean in and lower my voice. 'I have this dildo shoved up my ass, and I can't seem to get it out, Doc.'

'Danny.'

Her voice brooks no argument, and it's like an electrical charge to my balls. I chuckle as I straighten, loving the flash of annoyance in her amber eyes.

'I think this needs stitching.' I drag my arm from behind my back. Some blood has seeped through the bandage.

The fact I seem to have a legitimate reason to be here does not improve her mood. 'What did you do?'

'Cut it on some glass.'

She sighs. 'Fine. You're lucky we're in a lull right now. Follow me.'

Yes, ma'am. Fuck, I'd follow her right into hell at this particular moment.

I trail her ramrod frame as it briskly covers the distance to the nearest gurney. Even in slightly baggy scrubs, I can make out her ass, and I wonder if those pants just pull down. Her ponytail brushes between her shoulder blades in a hypnotic swing.

'Sit here.' She gestures to the empty gurney. 'I'll get some stuff and get Trisha started on the paperwork.'

She strides off again, and I watch her until she disappears, turned on by just the motion of her. I sit on the thin mattress and dangle my legs over the edge. The clinical smell of the place works deeper into my nostrils as I wait for Holly's return. I hear low voices, a grizzling baby, a mechanical pinging noise, and then she's back.

With equipment.

Bustling around, setting things up. I could watch her all night. Her quiet efficiency keeps my desire on a low simmer and my hard-on raging. I have no idea when efficiency became such a fuckin' turn on, but my dick is hard as stone watching her brisk, methodical movements. Or maybe it's just the scrubs and the stethoscope.

Finally she sits on a stool and uses her feet to roll it close to me as she snaps on some green gloves. The snap zips straight up my spine.

'Let's see it.' She holds out her hand, all business.

Lust churns in my gut, as does the urge to rile her up. 'You want me to pull the curtains, Doc?'

She shoots me a no-nonsense look. 'I think they'll be just fine open, thank you.'

I grin, and she ignores me as she quickly unwinds the bandage. She squirts some saline on the wound, which has stopped oozing now. She's quick and thorough as she wipes at the old blood with some gauze. Once it's clean, she angles the lamp to examine the cut. Luckily my tats don't extend to my forearms, which makes visualisation easier.

'What kind of glass was it?'

'Beer bottle.'

She gives a soft snort, and I suppress a smile as she inspects the site, her head bent over it, her profile glowing in the lamp light. Her hair smells sweet, like maple syrup, and my mouth waters. She shuts her eyes and feels inside and along the edges for what I assume might be retained glass fragments.

It's sore, but my balls ache worse as the V of her scrub top gapes a little, and the bell of her stethoscope brushes the slight swell of her cleavage. I want to play doctor with her so fucking bad.

She lifts her head. 'Probably needs four or five stitches.'

I smell coffee on her breath. 'Okay.'

'When did you last have a tetanus shot?'

'About two years ago with my last lot of stitches.'

She looks both curious about those stitches – left calf – and disappointed she's not going to get to jab me in the ass.

'I'll just wash up.'

She disappears, then comes back a couple of minutes later drying off wet hands. Within two minutes she's gloved and I'm draped, a patch of hair has been shaved around the site, and I'm all numbed up. She gets to work with the stitching, barely saying a word to me except for simple directions.

How can she be so cool when I'm running so fucking hot?

'So you were boozing?'

I laugh at her emphasis on boozing, like drinking's another sin she's added to the mental list she's compiling to keep me at bay.

'One beer at the end of the gig when this happened.' She sniffs a little, but doesn't make further comment.

'It might hurt to use your sticks the next few days.'

'I'll manage.' I dismiss her concern – it wouldn't be the first time I've played injured. 'Unless you want to come and supervise me. My own personal physician.'

The curved needle stops, poised above the ragged edges of the cut, and she glances up, the same flare of interest I'd seen in the elevator burning brief and bright before it's gone.

'Can't. Working the next three nights.'

I shrug. 'You're welcome any time.'

'Nights aren't good for me.'

Her eyes seem to say, *neither are you*. But I'm done with pansy-assed excuses. I know she wants me, I've just seen it in her eyes, for fuck's sake. 'Maybe I could give you a demo in the morning? You could drop in for breakfast. I make awesome pancakes.'

I don't know whether it's her hair, but I have maple syrup on the brain. I try not to think about pulling up that scrub top and pouring the sweet, sticky stuff all over her tits.

I am not in the least bit successful.

Her eyes flare a little more, as if she can see the pictures inside my head. 'No.' She lowers her gaze and pushes the needle through the skin. I feel a dull pressure, but nothing else.

'Mornings not good, either?'

She ties off the stitch and sighs, her frame losing some of its stiffness. 'I already told you, we can't do this.'

'Right. I'm not part of your plan.'

Sitting back, she looks at me directly. I try to keep my focus on her face and not the way the stethoscope nestles in that valley between the boobs I love so much.

'I have several more years left in my residency. If I pass. I'm having breakfast with my textbooks for the next few years.'

'So?' I shrug. 'Bring them with you. You gotta eat, right?'

She shakes her head. 'You don't understand. If I want to become an attending after my residency, I have to keep my head down and work and study. This stuff is hard.'

By which she implies being a drummer isn't. That's not true, of course, but it's not as hard as a medical degree I imagine.

'All I have is gaps, tiny slices of time here and there. I don't have hours or days to give anyone. And God knows I don't have the energy. I'd be a lousy partner. It's better to not even go there.'

Jesus. I've never heard anything sadder in my life. 'I'm not planning on adding to your burden of things to get through each day, Doc.' I smile at her because she looks weighed down just talking about it. 'I'm happy to fit into those gaps, and I'm not just talking about sex. I'm talking about fun. Stress relief. A foot rub, a hot bath, a cooked meal. Pillow talk if you want it. Someone to rant at when you've had a lousy day at work.'

Fucking hell. I sound like a complete sap. But even as the words tumble from my mouth, there's a resonance in them that settles into my bones like the dying notes of a cymbal swell shimmering gently into my marrow.

It should terrify me but it doesn't. I've known this woman is different from the first time I laid eyes on her. She looks terrified though because I'm clearly talking about more than fucking, which is no doubt an even greater threat to her life plan. Sex is one thing; foot rubs and feeding her is something else entirely.

So if I have to meet her where she's at right now, I will.

'Although screwing you until you can't see straight is also on offer.' I shoot her an easy grin. 'And you know what I can achieve in a short space of time.'

Her lips purse. Am I pushing too fast, too far? The glitter in her eyes tells me she's going to push back. 'Danny.' She glances over her shoulder and drops her voice when she returns her attention to me. 'Screwing a drummer is a really lousy career move.'

I chuckle. If she's trying to be insulting, it won't work. Plus I'm encouraged by that dirty word slipping from her pretty mouth. 'Haven't you heard, Doc? Screwing a drummer is always a great career move.'

She rolls her eyes and leans over my arm to continue her work. 'We come from different worlds.' Her voice stays low as I feel more dull pressure. 'Being with someone in my profession makes more sense. They'll understand the rigors of the job, the demands on my time.'

I know she's trying to discourage me but the fact she's even thinking about being with me is cause for celebration. Still, I keep it light. I don't want to scare the horses. 'Ah... I see. You only want to fuck doctors, huh?'

I suppose I should be jealous AF over that, but I know I can give her what she really needs. What she didn't know she needed.

Her hand falters as it pulls the thread through my skin. 'At least another doctor would understand why I'm always at work.' I can hear the certainty in her voice. 'And why even when I'm not at work, I'll probably still be totally preoccupied with it.'

I smile at that. I do like a challenge. 'That's only because you haven't had anything else to be preoccupied with, Doc. But I bet you my last cent, work has been the last thing on your mind since the' – I deliberately lean in closer to her and whisper – 'screwdriver.'

Her hand falters again as she ties off the suture. If she's thought about me half as much as I've thought about her, we're both in serious trouble.

She doesn't say anything, just puts in the last stitch, pulls the surgical drapes off my arm, and calmly applies a dressing. Only when she's done that does she look me in the eye, her expression serious. 'That isn't who I am, Danny. The woman in the elevator.'

'Oh, yes it is.' She just has to let her out.

'No.' Holly shakes her head. 'But thank you for... letting me be her, during the blizzard.' She stands and peels off her gloves, and her stethoscope gives that beautiful swing. 'I'll get one of the nurses to talk to you about wound care.'

Before I can stop her or call her back, she turns on her heel and walks away, and I crane my neck to follow her progress back down the corridor until she disappears into a room at the end. It looks like I'm going to need to prove to her she is the woman in the elevator. And that it's okay to have needs a medical calling alone cannot fulfil.

Challenge accepted.

* * *

Fifteen minutes later, my arm bandaged better than I'd managed it, I sign the paperwork. The local has worn off, and I've refused painkillers. The nurse accompanies me out, but someone calls to her, and I tell her I'll be fine. She smiles gratefully at me and turns away. I wait a beat or two, then slip silently down the darkened corridor in Holly's footsteps.

I have no idea if she's still down here somewhere, but it's all I've got. My boots sound loud on the linoleum floor, and I expect to have my ass busted at any moment. Suddenly, a door opens just ahead of me and I freeze. But it's her.

Holly.

My heart settles into an entirely different rhythm. She's halfway out the door when she spies me, her arms full of medical supplies, that goddamn stethoscope nestled exactly where I like it. The sign on the door says *supplies*. She gives me one of her cranky looks, and it has the predictable effect of throwing flame onto the smouldering heat of my desire.

'Danny!' She hisses my name and checks over my shoulder as I step close. 'What the hell are you doing back here? This is off limits to – non-medical personnel.'

But I see the flash in her eyes, hear the husky rasp of her breathing. And damn if the prissy way she says *non-medical personnel* doesn't yank me by the dick. I give her one of those slow smiles I know shows off my dimples and irritates her so much. I know because she frowns when I do it, just like she does now.

'You look hot as fuck in those scrubs, and that stethoscope is driving me nuts. I'm here to *do* you, Doc. For real this time – no imagination required. And I have a condom.'

I don't give her a chance to respond, just slide my hands onto her biceps and steer her back into the room. It's dark in here, too, but my eyes are adjusted enough to make out the looming shadows of row upon row of large, metallic shelves laden with stuff I can't identify and don't give a shit about. I only have eyes for Holly.

'Danny. We... shouldn't be doing this. I'm at work. Anyone can walk in here at any minute.'

'I know.' I smile as I direct her to the nearest row. 'That's half the thrill.'

'I... have patients.' But the catch in her voice betrays her excitement as I bump her back against the wall at the far end of the row.

'You're in a lull.'

I start unloading the stuff from her arms, shoving it haphazardly on the shelf beside me. She doesn't help, but she doesn't stop me either and, by the time she's empty-handed, her breathing is a rough pant winding its fingers around my cock, and I'm dizzy with it.

'I haven't been able to stop thinking about you.'

'Danny, I—'

I cut off whatever she's about to say with my mouth. I have to kiss her. And by the way she's melting against me, opening her mouth and clutching at my shirt, I'm guessing she has to kiss me, too. My hands slide to her hips as my tongue slides into her mouth, and she moans and twists her fingers into my shirt.

And Christ she feels good – hot and eager, greedy as her hands pull me closer. Every suck of my breath fills up with the sweetness of maple syrup. My pulse washes like a waterfall through my ears. My hands shake with need, the pain from my arm forgotten. She rubs against me, and I know how she feels. I want to bury myself inside her so bad.

To fuck her. Finally.

I pull away slightly, my lips not quite touching hers. 'Say you haven't been able to stop thinking about me.' I fully expect her to bite me, but I'm pathetically desperate to hear her articulate what her body already knows.

'I barely think of anything else,' she whispers.

I groan and kiss her hard instead of roaring and beating my chest like a fucking caveman, which is exactly what I want to do.

Holly Vincent is mine.

I drag the stethoscope off her neck as I pull at the hem of her scrubs and rip it up and off, her Henley following next. I vaguely note her bra is a pale pink as I fumble with the hooks. My hands shake with the need to be inside her. How I manage to get it off, I don't know. I'm juggling it and the stethoscope, all while her hands are working at the top button of my fly.

When she's completely topless I sling the stethoscope back around her neck. 'Jesus.' She's so fucking sexy like that, the bell and the earpieces brushing her tits. 'One of these days you and I are going to play doctor.'

Her breath hitches, then she's dragging me close again and whispering, 'Hurry,' against my mouth as she yanks down my fly.

I hurry. Grope for my wallet, pull out the condom, rip it open, knock her busy hands aside as I roll it on, all without breaking from the soft-hard seduction of her mouth. I am obsessed with her mouth. Its shape, the way it moves, the way it tastes. I want to spend hours kissing it. For damn sure I want to fuck it real bad. Hell, one day I'll write a song about it.

But not now.

Now my hands yank down her scrubs and her underwear, my hands slide under her ass and lift, pinning her to the wall with my hips as she locks her legs tight around my waist. I grab my cock and guide it to where she is so fucking hot and wet and ready for me.

'Yes!' Her gasp is soft in my ear as I tease her slick folds with my dick. 'There.'

I've almost forgotten in our haste that this is our first time, and I have a fleeting regret that it's up against a wall. It's not very romantic. But I'm too far gone to be a gentleman about it. And acutely aware I'm in a room full of medical supplies with a woman desperate for my cock, who probably knows how to perform a castration.

There'll be time enough for rose petals.

I pull back to look at her as I notch myself just inside her. She's gloriously naked except for her stethoscope, and I make sure our gazes are locked before I shove into her. She moans and her tits rock a little and I can tell it's 100 per cent better than anything she'd fantasised about in the elevator.

'I can fill in all your gaps, Holly.'

I pull out and thrust in again, and she gasps this time as she grasps my shoulder. I pick up the pace, thrusting and withdrawing, watching her head rock and her tits bounce. She's gorgeous, her chest rising and falling erratically, her eyes shut, her mouth parted.

I slide in to the hilt and it's 100 per cent better than I'd fantasised about. 'Let me fill them, Holly.'

Her amber eyes flick open. Even in the dark I can see they're roiling with lust, and I shove into her – hard. I withdraw quickly, and she moans again. 'I know you, Holly. I know you love it when I talk dirty. When I say *fuck*.' I thrust and withdraw. 'And *cock*.' Her nails bite into my neck at the profanity, and she pulses around me. My hips piston once more. 'And *pussy*.'

I go again and again. She whimpers, and her thighs tremble around my waist, her internal muscles contracting around my cock. I can tell she's close as my own pleasure balances on a knife's edge.

'I know you love it when I make you come.'

My hand slides between our bodies to her clit. It's as stiff as I am, and I flick it. She arches her back, bites her lip to stop from crying out, ploughs her fingers into my hair and twists until it physically hurts, but I don't care, I just kiss her. I kiss her like the world's about to end and I want to go out with her. Kiss her as I stroke her, kiss her as I fuck her deep and hard, kiss her as she fills my head with the sweet aroma of musk and maple syrup and the nonsensical sounds of her orgasm.

'Fuuuuck.' I groan, my scalp burning as I follow her into the light, my heart pounding, my body an agony of pleasure and pain, bucking and thrusting, until we're both spent and gasping against the wall.

I wait until her fingers loosen from my hair and slide bonelessly away and my pulse has settled a little and I can speak again. 'I can fill your gaps, Holly.' I pull back, lapping up the sight of her as I slide out. I ease her down until her feet touch the ground, shoving the condom in my pocket as I tuck myself away.

She blinks up at me, swaying a little like she can't really believe what's happened. I can hardly believe it, either.

'Let me be your respite, Holly.'

'Danny, I...'

I bend and kiss her, soft and brief. I don't expect an answer right now. 'Just think about it,' I whisper.

Then I turn and leave, certain that she'll be thinking of nothing else. Just like me.

# 7

## HOLLY

*Just think about it.*

Danny's words, what happened in the supply room, are all I *can* think about. It's been five days, but they play on repeat inside my head. Five days, during which I've fought the tug of those words. Five days where I've battled my body and something much deeper, denying them what they want.

*I can fill your gaps, Holly. Let me be your respite, Holly.*

Damn it all. I tell the man all I have is gaps, and he offers to fill them. He offers me respite. He couldn't have chosen his words better if he tried. If he'd said he wanted to fuck my brains out for eternity, he'd be much easier to ignore. Frankly, I don't need another person wanting something from me.

But he hadn't. He'd offered himself to me. In service to me. To be my port in the relentless storm that is my life. A place to lay my head and forget for a while in the snatches of time life affords me.

Those words are like music to my ears. Like drums. My ex had made everything about him, so Danny is a revelation.

And then there's the way he says *Holly*. It's cute and sexy when he calls me Doc, but holy cow, when he says Holly? Breathing it out like it's some kind of sacred word? Something precious? It weakens my knees and wraps glowing fingers around my heart.

But... I can't. No matter how tempted I am. There's only one thing worse than not throwing caution to the wind and taking Danny up on his offer. And that's the thought of taking it up and having him tire of filling my gaps because I'm boring and vanilla and always at work after three or six or twelve months.

And then he'll end it, which will be awful because my heart would be involved, and I don't need to be dealing with a broken one on top of everything else. Better to deny myself now, while I don't know what I'm missing, than let it drag on. Because he's absolutely right – there is more than fucking between us. No matter how much I try to deny it, the way my heart flip-flops when I see him is not normal.

Worse, I think he feels the same way.

Which is, of course, preposterous and will be ignored. I don't have time for a flip-floppy heart and I'm really good at denial. Even if just sitting here thinking about him has my nipples hard as bullets and an ache as jagged as the Rocky Mountains between my legs.

I have two precious days off, and I'm supposed to be studying. There are papers and open textbooks strewn across the coffee table. But all I can think about is Danny pounding me against the wall at work, me all but naked, and him all but clothed.

A sudden knock on my door startles me so much I actually jump a little. My pulse instantly accelerates. Danny? Could it be him? Maybe the cloud of oestrogen hanging around my apartment has finally reached him on the sixth floor, and he's decided to pay me a visit? To stop waiting for me to make the first move?

Eep!

Despite my resolve, I'm not sure I can resist another overture on his behalf and my pulse trips, and my legs tremble as I rise from the couch and head to the door. When I reach for the knob, my hand shakes. It's ridiculous how my body quakes, but it refuses to be quelled because it's him. I don't need to look through the peephole.

It's him. I know it is.

'Hey,' he says as the door swings open, cool and calm as you please, looking better than any man has a right to in jeans that cup and mould, in a sweater that clings and moulds, his dirty blond hair looking like it did after I'd twisted it all up when he was fucking me in the storeroom at work.

Sex hair.

My face warms thinking about how wanton I'd been. Was it only five nights ago? 'Hey.' My hey is far less cool and calm, my pulse tripping.

Shoving his shoulder casually into the jamb, his eyes rove over me like I'm wearing a string bikini instead of baggy track pants and an NYU T-shirt that is old and sloppy and faded and is currently sporting a coffee stain over the left boob area.

Of course.

Unperturbed, he holds up a grocery bag dangling from his fingers. 'Hungry?'

I have no idea what's in the bag and I hadn't been particularly hungry, but with him in my doorway I am suddenly ravenous. And not necessarily for food.

This is not good.

'I'm studying.' Must. Not. Get. Distracted. By. Hot. Drummer. With. Sex. Hair.

He shrugs, a smile lifting the corners of his mouth. 'Gotta eat though, right? Some carbs and protein to help you concentrate. And it's lunch time.'

'I... wasn't going to stop.' There's a bag of Cheetos with my name on it in the cupboard.

'No need to. You keep going – I'll cook. I'll plate up, I'll clean the kitchen and leave you to it. You won't even know I'm here.'

A smile plays on his mouth and I barely suppress my eyeroll. Like that was even remotely possible. 'You and I both know that if you cross this threshold there will be sex.'

He grins then, his blue gaze smug. So sure of himself. So cocky. The man is so damn easy in his skin it takes my breath away. He looks like he's never doubted himself in his life where I constantly overthink everything.

'Nope.' He shakes his head. 'This is the getting-to-know-you phase of our relationship. We're not doing sex.'

I blink at his bold pronouncement. Also... relationship?

His grin broadens. 'Don't look so disappointed, Doc. I'll start to think you only want me for my body.' Then he eases off the jamb and brushes past me into the apartment, the aroma of basil, bread and body – brash, swaggering, buff body – filling my senses.

'Chicken pesto pasta work for you?' he calls over his shoulder. 'Any allergies?'

My tummy rumbles as I stare at the space Danny had filled seconds prior, the empty corridor the only thing in my line of vision now. Sighing, I resign myself to the torture of him in my apartment, cooking for me, and shut the door.

Danny is hard to ignore as sizzling onions spice the air. The table from which I am working is only a few feet from where he slices and dices, my tea towel slung casually over his shoulder, which is hot in ways I wouldn't have thought possible.

He's as good as his word, not saying anything, just shuffling around, finding what he needs, dragging out pots and setting water to boil on the stove top, concentrating on the job at hand. But that doesn't mean he's not distracting as all giddy up. I'm supposed to be reviewing an anatomy subject, but Danny Colton's anatomy is far more interesting.

I wonder if I asked, would he strip off his clothes so I can study the flex and glide of what I know to be perfectly delineated muscles?

Sneaking glances as he works, I can see the shift of his biceps and triceps, the bunch of his deltoid, the undulation of his abdominals beneath the snug fit of his sweater. Combine that with mouth-watering aromas rising from the pan and Danny's utter competence in the kitchen and I've been staring at the same page since he entered.

By the time a bowl of chicken pesto pasta drizzled with olive oil and topped with cheese is in front of me, I've taken very little in, not even the cursor that blinks at me from the laptop screen.

'For you, ma'am,' he murmurs with a cheeky little bow and a flourish of his hands. 'Get that into you.'

He smiles at me and I can't help but smile back. I didn't know I had such a thing for competence, but a man who can cook is ticking all my boxes. Add to that fix a heating problem, mend some rotting stairs and dish out a handful of orgasms and I'm going full kink.

'I made plenty extra,' he says as he heads back to the sink and flicks on the faucet. 'Enough for a couple of takeout containers so you have some meals in the fridge ready to go the next few days.'

Well... hell. Not fair. Good to look at, excellent with his hands and considerate.

He squeezes detergent into the water and I realise I'm being rude. The man just cooked for me; the least I can do is show some appreciation. 'Danny... stop.' I reach across the table and grab up the mess of papers. 'Sit,' I say, stacking them in a neat-ish pile on top of the textbooks, which I push to one side. 'Grab some. Eat with me.'

'Nah.' He shakes his head. 'I'll just clean up and leave you to your study.'

I sigh. His understanding only makes me feel shittier about ignoring him. Or trying to, anyway. 'Come on, please? I should take a proper break from all this so why not join me?'

I suddenly feel desperate that he doesn't leave. Having him here in my kitchen has been distracting, yes, but also quite... homey? Something I haven't realised I've been missing. I've lived by myself for the past two years, and the company – having someone nearby indulging in the purely domestic duty of cooking a meal – has been unexpectedly nice.

It reminds me of doing my homework around the dinner table with my brother and sister, my father – the chef in our house – whipping up something delicious smelling, my mother helping us if needed in between packing orders for her Tupperware gig she did for years to bring in extra money to our barely-getting-by household.

Having Danny in my kitchen, I realise, feels like family.

'Well, it looks pretty good, even if I do say so myself,' he says with a slow smile, then reaches into the wall cupboard and grabs a bowl.

I take my first bite of pasta as he sits his ass in the chair opposite me so I won't ogle the way his jeans pull taut across his quads. And I am in gastronomic heaven. Earthy flavours of garlic, onion and basil mix with the tartness of lemon, the sharpness of parmesan and the succulent juiciness of the chicken, which practically melts in my mouth.

My eyes flutter closed on a low, satisfied moan. I can't help myself. It's that good. As they flutter open again, I find his eyes on me, on my mouth, and everything inside me shivers in the best kind of way. 'Mmm,' I murmur after I align enough brain cells to form words. 'Amazing.'

I expect some kind of smug, cocky rejoinder, but he merely nods. 'Good. Eat up.'

I shove my fork into the bowl. 'How's the arm?' I ask as I spear pasta. He's pushed his sweater sleeves up and I can see the small adhesive dressing that covers his sutures.

'All good. I have an appointment in a few days to get the stitches out.'

I nod as I take my first bite and then I don't say anything else. It's delicious and I devour it in no time at all. I am done and his bowl is still half full. I give an embarrassed half laugh as I place my fork in the bowl. 'Sorry, I was hungrier than I thought.'

He shakes his head. 'Don't apologise. I like a woman who knows how to eat.'

My insides loop-the-loop at his suggestive words and I search his gaze for any sexual innuendo, but he returns his attention to his food with only the merest smile tugging at his mouth. 'Where'd you learn to cook like that?'

Danny smiles around a mouthful of pasta. 'Bob.'

I blink. 'Bob?'

I know they're related but I didn't realise Danny and Bob knew each other that well. The older man had never mentioned Danny prior to him arriving, although I suppose whilst friendly, Bob isn't exactly chatty.

'How? I'm pretty sure he has Uber Eats on speed dial.' I've spoken to enough drivers on their way to Bob's apartment to assume that cooking isn't one of his skills.

Danny shrugs. 'It's harder to be motivated when you're cooking for one.'

Oof. Isn't that the truth? When do I ever cook for myself? Properly cook, like Danny has cooked for me today? 'Yeah.'

As if he knows I'm talking about myself he asks, 'Do you cook?'

I laugh at the suggestion. Cooking takes time I don't have. 'I'm more into food... construction.'

'Oh yeah?' He raises two eyebrows. 'What does that mean?'

'It means taking several pre-packaged items and putting them together to form another dish. Like some corn chips, a jar of salsa and a handful of cheese. Throw it in the microwave for a couple of minutes and hey presto – nachos.'

He winces a little like I've just insulted Mexico. 'Bad nachos.'

I shrug. 'It takes three minutes. I'll eat gourmet after I become an attending.'

Of course I know better than most about the health benefits of good nutrition and fuelling my body properly, but I'm also perpetually busy and tired. Eating has become more about function than indulgence.

He shoots me a piteous look but doesn't push. 'Bob has a four-dish repertoire which he claims is all you need for an evening meal. This.' He stabs his fork at the bowl. 'Fried rice. Beef stroganoff and shepherd's pie. But he also taught me how to make eggs and pancakes because they're a breakfast thing.'

'Oh.' I blink again. So they do know each other well? 'You're close, then?'

'I lived with him for a couple of years before I went to college.'

More blinking. Danny went to college?

'My father, who died when I was a baby, he was Bob's cousin and I probably only saw him briefly every few years or so. But when my mother got remarried – for the third time – when I was fifteen and I didn't want to go to buttfuck Arizona with her and Waldo the wonderful, he offered me a place here.'

The derision in Danny's voice tells me he has history with his mom's husbands. 'That was... good of him.'

'Poor bastard.' Danny shakes his head and laughs. 'His wife had died ten years before I came on the scene and they'd had trouble in the pregnancy department, including having a stillborn baby, so they'd never had kids of their own. He had no idea how to look after a teenager with a chip on his shoulder and an appetite that wouldn't quit, but he just game-planned me like I was a military mission to accomplish. He was no gourmet but insisted a person only needed a few dishes to get by and that every guy needed to know how to cook. Compared to my mom who could burn water, it was a revelation.'

It's way more than I want to know but I realise in his telling that I've assumed a lot about this cocky young guy who looks at me in such a direct way, and I don't like that about myself one little bit. Not only had Danny gone to college but he'd never known his father and been shunted to a relative he barely knew as a teenager when his mother moved on.

Is it any wonder he had a chip on his shoulder? He doesn't appear to have one now, but I wonder if the band and the tatts were a consequence of that time in his life.

My flip-floppy heart flipped and flopped again.

'That's how you know how to fix stuff?'

Danny nods. 'Pretty much. I used to help him on his jobs. Which is why he knows I'm capable of handling the building while he's away on his Reno trip.'

'Does Bob ever win anything on these extended gambling adventures?'

A laugh bursts from his mouth. 'I doubt it. I think it's more a camaraderie thing, for him. Meeting up with old buddies, shooting the shit.' Danny shrugs. 'Whatever. He deserves it. He's a good guy. He's been good to me.'

I nod. 'It sounds like it.'

'He also bought me my first drum kit.'

'So I have him to thank for the racket?'

A sharp laugh escapes his throat as his eyes twinkle – freaking twinkle – at me. 'Him and rock and roll. Sorry about that.'

He doesn't look remotely sorry as I wave his apology away with a flap of my hand.

'What's your band's name?'

Danny takes a mouthful, which he bites, chews and swallows before he answers. 'The first band I ever joined when I was eighteen was Garage Nights. The music wasn't bad but we didn't really like each other much outside of the band. The one after that was Penny for Them and the one after that was Gunpowder and Lace. My current band is Neon Dicks.'

I laugh even as I wonder if four bands in a decade means he doesn't play well with others or he moves around a lot. 'Colourful.'

His lips twitch. 'We thought so.'

'Any good?'

He smiles, oozing that confidence I have come to know so well. Everything about that smile, that demeanour, says *whatdaya reckon?*

'I think you know how good I am with a stick.'

Heat warms my face and I squirm. A stick. Other inanimate objects...

'We're not about to play at Madison Square Garden,' he continues with a shrug as he loads up another forkful, 'but we have a good local following. Enough gigs to get by, which is not nothing.'

I suppose it's not and I have no idea how talented Danny really is or how tough it is out there to be a musician, but... the fact he doesn't seemed bothered by such a loosey-goosey life plan is a revelation.

'And you're okay with that?'

He laughs at my question and I realise that I may have come across as questioning his ambition, which I guess I am. But... who lives like that? I have goals for the next decade. Short term. Medium term. Long term. They're listed in a bullet journal I started on my first day of med school, and I continuously update.

Another shrug. 'It'll do for now.'

God... imagine. Imagine living life with so little clear direction. My chest tightens at the thought. But something else loosens at the allure of it.

'You don't approve?' he says.

The side of his mouth kicks up like he doesn't give a rat's ass whether I approve or not. As he shouldn't. If Danny wants to half-ass his life, he's perfectly entitled. 'Not my business.'

'But you know what you want and where you're heading, right? You have direction.'

'Sure.' I nod. 'I'm specialising in emergency medicine.'

'You plan on staying here or do you want to take those skills somewhere big, like New York or Chicago?'

I shake my head. 'No. I want to go rural.'

He blinks like I've finally surprised him. 'Rural?'

'Yes,' I say stiffly.

As ever, I'm defensive over my choice just like I'd always been with my ex, who'd never taken my career aspirations seriously. Why is it so hard to believe that I would want to take my skills to a place screaming out for them?

New York and Chicago have a plethora of emergency medicine specialists.

'Do you know how inadequately staffed and resourced our rural hospitals are? How hard it is to attract skilled doctors? Which means rural people get an inferior service. That's grossly inequitable. And—' I fix him with a steely stare. 'That means rural people are sicker and sometimes they die completely unnecessarily because they turn up to an ER in a critical condition and there's only an inadequately trained doctor who's scared witless.'

The room is silent for long beats as he regards me seriously. 'What happened?' he asks quietly.

I open my mouth to deny that anything happened. But there's compassion in his blue, blue gaze and it's like he sees me. Something my ex never did. It makes me want to tell him.

'My grandmother. She died. After a car accident on a rural road. I still remember my mother getting that phone call.' I shudder as her wailing comes back to me now.

'How old were you?'

'Almost fourteen.'

'You were close?'

'Very.'

I smile as I think about my grandmother and how she was my *Gilmore Girls* buddy, watching along with me, always with some freshly popped corn, drooling over Luke in an exaggerated way because she knew how much it scandalised me.

'She ended up in an ER with only one junior doctor who was out of his depth and didn't act quickly enough. I've seen the autopsy. She could have lived if he'd known what to do or if he'd evac'd her earlier to somewhere that did.'

'I'm sorry.'

I shake my head. It's not his fault. But his apology is surprisingly heartfelt. 'Thank you.'

'So, that's what motivates you to push yourself?'

'Yeah.' I nod. 'I know I can't save everybody but...'

'You can try.'

I nod again. He does see me. 'Right.'

'Well, I think that's amazing.'

Danny's quick, easy compliment goes straight to my head. 'My ex thought it was self-indulgent.' I don't know why I share this titbit of information. The topic, I suppose. But it's out before I can call it back.

'Your ex?'

'Warren.' Even the name sets my teeth on edge. How did I let myself and what I wanted, become so subsumed by his career and what *he* wanted? I'd mistakenly thought there was room for both our careers in his future. 'We were together for a few years during med school. He's training to be a plastic surgeon.'

'A guy who's going to spend his days doing boob jobs thinks what you're doing is self-indulgent?'

I laugh out loud. 'Yes.'

'What a douchebag.'

I laugh again. 'Yup.' Warren really was a douchebag.

'What happened with him?'

Now that was a long and sorry saga, but luckily easily summed up. 'He always joked that I'd follow him to LA where he was going to make a fortune nipping and tucking. And then I realised he was serious.'

'Total douchebag.'

'He is, yes. Thankfully I woke up to myself and—'

'Dumped his ass?'

I smile. 'Something like that.' He hadn't taken it well – Warren could be cruel – but my blinkers had been well and truly ripped off. 'What about you?' I ask as Danny's eyes blaze with sympathy. I don't need or want his sympathy. I'm good. I'm back on track. 'Any douche exes?'

'No.' He shakes his head. 'I've had a few semi-serious girlfriends but none that have lasted long enough to class as an ex.'

I almost laugh out loud – of course. Why would this guy, who is God's gift to vaginas, tie himself down to one woman? 'So you just have... groupies?'

I have no clue why I blurt that out. The idea of Danny having groupies shoots a hot streak of jealousy through my gut. But everyone knows it's the drummers who get the groupies. I've literally spent the last decade of my life with my head in some textbook or other and even I know that.

His gaze is steady as it meets mine, a touch of humour lurking. 'Sure.'

'Have you slept with any of them?'

Why am I asking this? *Whyyyy?* I don't want to know this stuff. It's none of my business who Danny Colton sleeps with, plus, I really don't want to know. But I can't stop myself from asking either.

'Occasionally.' He quirks an eyebrow. 'Does that bother you?'

'No.' Except it really does.

Clearly not convincing him one iota, he laughs. 'Okay, sure.'

I fold my arms, hating how he sees right through me, hating that he sees how much the thought of him sleeping with anonymous women itches under my skin. 'I guess that's a hard lifestyle to give up.'

Slowly, Danny shakes his head as if he's realising this isn't just me being flippant. Something I'm only just realising, too. 'I'm not sixteen any more, Doc. My oats are sewn. Being a one-woman man sounds pretty damn good to me.'

My heart skips a beat, my stomach clenches, my ovaries bloom. Freaking bloom. What the actual fuck is happening right now? 'Monogamy, Danny?' From the guy who has no exes because he never stays with one woman long enough?

I shoot him my best *pfft, really?* look, but he just holds my gaze and calmly replies, 'Yes, Holly. Monogamy.'

My breath catches at his earnestness. 'That doesn't seem very rock and roll.'

'Fuck rock and roll. After three stepdaddies, I know how easy it is for some people to walk away from commitments and promises. And I know what it's like to be at the shitty end of that. I've never made any woman I've slept with any promises because I knew when I did, I was going to keep them.'

He is deadly serious, and I believe him, the conviction in his eyes holds me in the palm of his hand. Dear God, I want this man so freaking hard right now I can barely see straight. And not just his body. But his whole, big, beautiful, righteous soul. I'm actually a little breathy from the force of his sincerity.

Breaking eye contact like he hasn't just permanently realigned my chakras, he returns his attention to his bowl of pasta and I sit and watch as he forks food into his mouth and swallows. I watch until it's all gone, my body humming, my brain cells buzzing.

Uttering a satisfied sigh, he lifts his eyes and meets mine. 'I'll clean up and get out of your hair.'

He stands, whisks up my bowl and strides to the sink. I don't argue with him or offer to help, I just let him get on with it as I open my laptop, sort through the pages, find my place in the textbooks. But I'm as aware of him as I am of my own heartbeat. Danny at my sink. Danny with sudsy hands. Danny dividing up leftovers into containers.

Danny in my life like he's always been there.

When he's done, he crosses back to me and I am excruciatingly aware of every footfall as his bulk lumbers closer and closer, his crotch at my eye level as he pulls to a halt. My pulse fires erratically as he looms over me and I look up as his mouth touches down where my hairline meets my forehead.

'Don't forget to take regular breaks to stretch,' he murmurs as he pulls away.

Before I can say anything, he turns and strides to the door and opens it before I even register his intent. 'Thanks for lunch,' I call after him as the door clicks shut.

I am once again alone but, with my heart glowing warm and soft, I am not lonely. I am a strong, independent woman, but I cannot deny, Danny taking care of me just now?

That's not nothing.

# 8

## DANNY

I bide my time for another five days because I don't want to rush Holly or come on too hard, too fast. I learned a lot about her the other day. About why she's so driven and why she doesn't see herself with someone whose future isn't mapped out for the next few decades.

A quick fuck in a closet at her work, sure. Something long term? Not so much.

I know I'm different. Not in her wheelhouse. But I also know, in that way I just seem to know this woman, that I tempt her to want something outside her wheelhouse. Maybe for the first time in her life.

And I don't want to screw that up by crowding her.

Because, and I know it's crazy after knowing her such a short period of time, I'm 100 per cent gone for her. Bob told me years ago when I'd visited him as a kid that he'd fallen for Linda the first time he'd laid eyes on her, and there was something in the way he'd said it that left me in no doubt.

And, despite the rather chaotic ups and downs of my mother's love life and the sex-in-bathroom-stalls groupie hook-ups that are a part of band life, I truly believe that for some people there is one special person.

I just never believed I was one of those people. Until now.

Which is why I gotta play this smart. Holly's not a groupie who just wants to brag to her friends she blew a Neon Dick in a restroom in a bar – doesn't really matter which one of us; we're kinda interchangeable to a lot of women.

Which is fine. I have been the very happy recipient of such slavish devotion to the band and it's not like I'm taking names and numbers after, either.

Holly has a life plan and I'm good with that, too. I don't want to derail the course of her life, but I'm thinking I'd kinda like to sit in the seat beside her and share the ride. And, if I have any hope of convincing Holly of that, I need to play it cool.

So, she needs to miss me. A little. Enough that she can't understand why she can't stop thinking about me. And there has to be absolutely zero sex. I was serious when I told her that this was the getting-to-know-you part of our relationship. I want Holly to know that I'm not knocking on her door to get my end away because she's convenient.

Do I want to bang the ever-loving fuck out of Holly Vincent? Hell yes. Knowing she's so close and how good we are together has been pure torment. God knows, I've jacked off to the image of her stethoscope against her tits so much I'm surprised my cock hasn't fallen off.

But I don't want just sex from her. I want, *tell me all about your childhood.* And, *what's your deepest darkest secret?* And, *what's your zombie apocalypse plan?* I want to know everything. I want to spend the rest of my life knowing Holly Vincent.

And nobody ever died of blue balls.

But it's been five days and I can't go any longer without seeing her. Even if she slams the door in my face, at least I'll have seen her. I saw her this morning at quarter to six, but it was at a distance so it doesn't count. And no, I wasn't stalking her, I just happened to be coming in from walking Mrs Cameron's poodle as she drove out of the parking garage.

She didn't see me because it wasn't quite daylight yet and she was concentrating on the road, but with her hair in that neat ponytail and her hospital ID around her neck, she was definitely off to work. Which means, at eight-thirty, she should be home by now, right?

I'm not quite sure what time her shift finishes, but I know from TV shows they pull long ones in the ER. So... I guess there's only one way to find out.

Light flickers under her door as I approach and I can hear the low murmur of music, or maybe the TV. She's home. My dumb heart leaps at the thought, and I don't hesitate to knock. Maybe she doesn't want company after a long day, but... maybe she does?

The door opens and Holly is standing there rugged up in her duvet, not dissimilar to the way she'd been rugged up the day she'd bashed on my door all cranky about her thermostat. My dick has a very Pavlovian response to that even though the only bare skin I can see are her face and her hands.

I blink. 'Is your heating broken again?' I cast a glance over her shoulder into the darkened living room. There's no waft of frigid air.

She shakes her head. 'No. It's just... cosy like this.'

The way she says *cosy* has my spidey senses prickling. Why does she need cosy? There's a tiny V between her brows and although the dark makes it hard to ascertain, I think she's red and puffy around her eyes. My gut tightens. 'Everything okay?'

She shakes her head slowly, her lips pressed together, and although I can't see them, I think her shoulders just slumped under the duvet. 'Long, rough day at work.'

Did something specific happen? Something tragic? I suppose that's the downside of being a doctor. Of working in the ER.

'My feet are killing me. I got a parking ticket. And my period. And there's no chocolate in the apartment.'

I blink at the litany of misery as I try to figure out whether her telling me deeply personal stuff is a good sign or a bad one. I don't think I've ever been with a woman who wasn't a friend who's just blurted out stuff about her period.

Oh God... has she already friend-zoned me?

The thought is not a welcome one and I refuse to give it any space in my head. But I know a lot is riding on how I react and what I do in these next moments. It's a test. Not from Holly but from the universe. One I intend to pass with flying colours. One that, when she's better, will make Holly realise that I'm life-partner material.

'Okay, well...' I pull out my phone and navigate to a delivery app. 'We can get chocolate in any kind of way you want it delivered. Block, brownies, fudge.'

For a split second, Holly's face almost crumples, but she pulls herself back from that edge, nodding and sniffling. 'Block. But...' Her voice is soft like she's too miserable to even project it. 'Brownies would be kinda nice.'

'Block and brownies it is,' I say as I step inside her apartment.

Holly falls back and I smile at her as my thumb sweeps over the keyboard. I nudge the door shut with my foot and slip my arm around her shoulder as she shuffles to the couch.

The TV is playing a *Gilmore Girls* re-run, the nearby coffee table is covered in several scrunched-up tissues and a hot water bottle is sitting in the middle.

She ignores it as she snuggles down into the folds of the squishy fabric couch, lying on her side, her legs drawn up, her face pale now I can see it properly thanks to the light being thrown from the television.

'Does that need some more hot water in it?' I ask.

Holly nods. 'Yes, please.'

Right. Good, I can do that. I can't magic away a parking ticket or period cramps or the sadness of a day – a long, rough day – but I can get her chocolate. And I can shove a hot water bottle in a microwave.

Busying myself, I do just that. The app tells me chocolate is fifteen minutes away, so it's just me and the water bottle between Holly and despair right now. The microwave dings and I grab the object, now living up to the hot part. I sit at the end of the couch and offer it to Holly. 'Let me know if it's not hot enough.'

Rolling onto her back, Holly stretches out her legs as she unfurls herself from the duvet like a butterfly emerging from a chrysalis, no more looking like a puffy pinata. She's in a pair of leggings, a sweater and thick socks. The soles of her feet are a whisker away from brushing the side of my thigh as she performs a half sit up to take the hot water bottle.

Collapsing back against the couch, she presses the bottle low on her belly, shutting her eyes on a deep sigh. 'God... that's good.'

I'm relieved that a rubber bag full of hot water seems to be supplying some respite, but surely in this day and age women shouldn't have to put up with feeling this shitty. 'Is there some medication you can take?'

'Already done. It's better.' She tucks her legs up again, gathering the duvet back over her as she turns on her side.

I stare at her in the low light, cocooned in her cosy chrysalis once again. *This* is better? She'd been down here going through this all by herself while I dithered about wondering how long I should wait.

Jackass.

Sure, she's no doubt used to doing this alone, but that doesn't mean she should have to, right? It seems to me since her douche ex, Holly's been determined to not lean on anyone. 'You okay if I stay for a bit?'

Eloise – the girlfriend of Nick, the bass player – once told me that when she was having bad cramps she wished she had the power to just explode men with one stabby look from her eyeballs. Maybe me being here with Holly is actually the last thing she wants and she's too wrung out to object.

'If you can make chocolate appear asap you can stay as long as you like,' she murmurs, her gazed fixed on the TV.

Okay, not exactly a ringing endorsement on my presence but I'll take it.

We watch TV then. I sense she's not in the mood for chatter so I don't try to initiate conversation. I just watch quietly until the end credits roll ten minutes later and the door intercom rings. I rise to buzz the delivery guy up, greeting him when he arrives and relieving him of the brown paper back carrying emergency period chocolate.

When I return to the couch, Holly has already hauled herself upright, her back to the arm of the couch, her legs thrust out in front of her. She has the duvet more loosely draped, unwrapping it from around her head and allowing her arms out. The television has been turned down so it's now only a low murmur.

She makes grabby hands at me and I chuckle as I hand the bag over. Opening it, she thrusts her face into the bag and inhales deeply. 'Oh God.' She groans as she glances up at me. 'Just the smell is enough to make me feel better.'

'Good to know.'

I resume my seat at the end of the couch and enjoy the show of Holly ripping into the wrapper around the block of chocolate – one of three I ordered – snapping off two rows and crunching them down like they were carrots sticks instead of something that is usually savoured. She snaps off two more before she seems to remember that I am also in the room.

'Want some?' she asks around her next mouthful.

I shake my head, bemused. 'I'm good, thanks.' I couldn't possibly deprive her.

She smiles so big at me it's like someone has turned on the light. Clearly that was the right answer. Once those two rows are gone, she delves into the bag again and hauls out a plastic container with a half dozen brownies. Ripping off the lid, she helps herself to one, her teeth sinking into the square, and the noise she makes at the back of her throat and the way her eyes shut is exactly the way they shut when I made her come in the elevator.

Like she's experiencing next-level ecstasy, and hell if I don't feel that right down to my throbbing balls. Who knew watching a woman inhale chocolate-based food like it was an Olympic sport was such a turn on?

'This is so freaking good,' she says, her eyes opening and finding mine, her voice muffled as she tries to chew, swallow and speak. 'You really should try this.'

Again, I decline. I'd rather watch her, listen to those appreciative noises spilling from lips coated with crumbs. 'I'm enjoying the show.'

She rolls her eyes at me but doesn't stop eating until three brownies have disappeared. It's barely been ten minutes since I handed the bag over but it appears she's finally indulged in enough chocolate to satisfy the dictates of her hormones.

Shoving one hand on her stomach just above the hot water bottle, she grabs a tissue from the box and wipes at her mouth before tossing it on the table to join the others. Sighing contently, she scooches back down, her head propped on the arm, her legs extended, her feet, which now peek out of the end of the duvet, once again almost touching my thigh.

I quirk an eyebrow. 'Good?'

Another sigh. 'So good.'

'Better?'

'Much.' She smiles. 'Thank you. You're really good at providing food.'

Hell, yeah I am. And I want that to continue. 'You know what else I'm really good at? Not,' I add quickly when I realise that sentence could be miscon-strued, 'sex.'

What kind of a dude could witness Holly's current state and think, *I know what she wants – some dick banging around in there.*

Her mouth quirks up at one side. 'Although you are really good at that.'

I grin. Hell fucking yeah I am. Her compliment goes straight to my head – both of them – but I'm not dumb enough to think that's some kind of invita-tion. I have zero issues with period sex, it's just not the vibe she's putting out right now.

'I give a really great foot massage, too.'

She half laughs. 'Of course you do. Danny Colton, fairy godmother.'

I groan this time in a fake horrified manner, like she's insulted my manhood. That sounds depressingly platonic. 'Thank you. I think?' I glance at her socked feet. 'Shall I?'

'You have to now. You can't boast about your prowess and not follow through.'

She's right. I cannot. Nor do I have any intention of not following through.

Grinning, I pull off the sock on the left foot and move my ass a little closer so her heel rests on top of my thigh. She places the other foot flat to the floor and I ignore how it opens her legs. With the duvet covering most of her lower half, it's not like she's flashing me.

Placing one hand on the sole of her foot, one hand on the top, I stroke from toes to heel and back up again, using firm, even pressure.

'Oh dear Lord.' Her eyes flutter closed and she lets out a long, slow exhale, which tells me all I need to know about her state of bliss. 'I think every woman should have a Danny when she's on her period.'

'I take it your ex wasn't much of a foot rubber.'

She snorts. 'The only thing he liked to massage was his ego.'

Supressing a laugh, I try not to feel superior as my fingers work her toes from the front and behind and we don't speak for a few minutes. Her eyes stay shut and she whimpers pleasurably while I rub her feet and I concentrate on my hands while willing my cock to not even think about twitching.

'So, come on then,' I say after she moans a particularly lusty moan and my dick is about to mutiny. 'Tell me about this day of yours.'

Maybe she doesn't want to talk about it. Maybe she can't. But I'm not going to be some bullshit chicken-ass too afraid, or too full of my own importance, to ask.

She sighs as her eyes flutter open and lock on mine. 'I don't know where to start.'

I nod slowly. Her days must be pretty full on. I glance at my hands as they knead her instep, giving her time to gather her thoughts. 'Did something happen?'

'Apart from not being fast enough to dodge a flying fist you mean?'

My fingers stop the massage abruptly and my gaze flies to hers. 'Someone hit you?'

She shrugs. 'It happens occasionally. Occupational hazard.'

'What?' The hot hiss of fury roils in my gut, broiling the contents.

'It's fine. It was an old woman with Alzheimer's who was flailing around while we were trying to restrain her from running out into the street. I'm crankier with myself more than anything. Usually I see them coming and I can duck.'

Seriously? What the fuck. She seems so calm about it. Like she works at a boxing ring instead of a hospital. 'Did she hurt you?'

'Nah, just a glancing blow near my ear. Didn't even leave a mark.'

I blink at her casual dismissal of violence in the workplace. 'Still... didn't it piss you off? You shouldn't have to put up with that kind of thing.'

'Sure, at the time it was a bit of a shock and I wasn't exactly thrilled about being beaned by a little old lady, but...' She shrugs again. 'It wasn't deliberate. She has dementia. The world's a scary place for her. She was just scared.'

Her gaze is soft and her voice forgiving, and I marvel at that. 'You're a good person.'

'Then why have you stopped massaging my foot?' she asks with a smile as she wriggles it in my loose grasp.

I smile back and recommence. 'What else?' I ask as my fingers dig into her arch, eliciting a soft moan. I have a feeling being smacked upside the head was just one of the things Holly had to contend with today.

She sighs but it's heavier this time and I sense that this is the thing weighing most on her mind as she stares at my hands working her feet. 'There was this man. Ninety-two. End-stage cancer. Double pneumonia. In a really bad way. Knew it was the end. I didn't know him but he'd been treated by oncology at the hospital on and off for over a decade. He already had an NFR in place but there was no next of kin, no loved one with him; he came in from home in the back of an ambulance. Sweet old guy apologising for making such a fuss. He said he thought he was okay to go at home but that when it got down to it, he didn't want to die alone.'

She takes a ragged breath which is so loaded with empathy I feel it as a physical weight against my skin. 'So he came to us.' She shakes her head and glances at me, her eyes glassy. 'There were no beds in oncology and I knew he wasn't going to last that long anyway. So we made him comfortable and took it in turns to hold his hand. He died a few hours later. But it's so sad. He died surrounded by strangers. It's just not right, is it?'

It's fair to say that I feel wholly inadequate in this moment to be a comfort. I'm a drummer, FFS. I know how to beat a stick against something percussive. And I can massage her feet – that's it. Maybe her ex knew what to say? The thought of that has me spurting out the first thing that comes into my head. 'He wasn't alone though, was he? He had you guys.'

Which is actually pretty damn good.

'It's not the same,' she says dismissively.

'Maybe not to you. But if he's been in and out of hospital for a decade and he has no significant others, maybe you weren't strangers. Maybe you were... home to him.'

A tear spills from one eye and tracks down her cheek before she dashes it away. 'Yeah.' She sniffles. 'Maybe you're right. I hope so.' She rubs at her face. 'Sorry. I know working in ER is what I want but sometimes I think I'm far too soft to work there.'

'Don't.' I shake my head. Holly shouldn't have to apologise for shedding tears over the death of an old man who'd found his way into her ER today because he didn't want to die alone. She should be wearing that shit like a badge of honour. 'I'd rather a doctor who has empathy than one who doesn't.'

She gives a husky half laugh as she switches feet. 'My boss would beg to differ.'

Bending her knee, she pushes the toes of the first foot under my thigh. A flaming arrow of lust shoots north about three inches and buries itself between my balls. Her other foot lands in my waiting hands.

'Well,' I say as I ignore the fire in my crotch and pull off her sock, 'he sounds awful.' What the world needs is more doctors who empathise with their patients, not medical automatons.

'She,' Holly corrects. 'And yes. She can be. Although I suppose she's just trying to toughen us up. There's a time for emotion. I've gotta learn to compart-mentalise.'

I press my thumb into the centre of her arch, and Holly shudders as her eyes close again and she lets out a long low moan which, thank fuck, stops all that nonsense talk about compartmentalising.

It also does all kinds of crazy things to my pulse and the tightness of my testicles.

'Jesus, Danny. You should do this for a living. Your fingers are magic.'

I laugh. I've been doing all kinds of fancy stick moves since I first learned how to hit a drum, which makes them extra dextrous. And I give her the full treatment, kneading and stroking until her audible appreciation quietens then stops, and I'm pretty sure she's actually fallen asleep. Her deep, even breathing seems to confirm it.

I don't know whether that's a good thing or a bad thing, but she looks a helluva lot better than when I arrived an hour ago. Her face has smoothed out. There's no frown lines now; in fact, she looks years younger.

Easing her foot off my lap, I gently remove the hot water bottle from her stomach and pad over to the microwave to give it another quick zap. When it beeps I remove it and walk it back, repositioning it before tucking the duvet around her.

The heat from the bottle must finally have seeped through because she stirs as I turn to go. 'I'm sorry,' she murmurs, her voice low, her eyelids fluttering open and closed. 'I fell asleep on you.'

'It's fine,' I whisper, although I don't know why I'm whispering. Maybe it's the overall ambience of the dark room and flickering TV glow. 'Go to sleep. I'll see myself out.'

She nods and says, 'Thank you,' a small smile on her mouth as her eyes drift shut again. I smile at her rugged up, her face almost beatific now. I'm feeling pretty damn smug as well as privileged to be the one that made a difference for her tonight.

'Danny?'

Her voice drifts to me as I reach for the doorknob, and I pause. 'Yes?'

'I promise I don't always look like a doctor or a bridge troll. One of these days I hope you get to see me all glammed up instead of wearing a duvet and stuffing my face like the Cookie Monster.'

Is she kidding? I've seen her naked – I'll take that any day. 'Cookie Monster is hot,' I throw over my shoulder.

She laughs and says, 'Weirdo.'

But it sounds sleepy and I call, 'Goodnight,' and close the door behind me.

# 9

## HOLLY

I can't quite believe I'm here as I stand slightly back and separate from the crowd. This isn't my usual scene but here I am anyway because I can't stop thinking about Danny, damn it.

Lights strobe and pulse around the dance floor area, which is off to one side of the bar. It's not a big space but there's a lot of people all packed in tight and standing like it's a mosh pit despite the stage only being raised a foot or so off the floor. Bodies move to the beat, eyes glued on the band, arms lifted as if trying to catch the music in their fingers as its blasts around them.

There's a distinct smell that wafts from the wall of bodies all perspiring under hot lights. Spilled booze and the sickly-sweet aroma of weed and cherry ChapStick vapes clinging to fabric already sporting pit stains. Throw in the clash of dozens of different perfumes and colognes and it is a unique smell.

Not bad. But raw and earthy, adding to the almost feral atmosphere as the human mass shifts up and down and side to side as one moving beast.

Like a herd of shuffling, grasping zombies.

It's an epidemiological nightmare. People squeezed tight, skin on skin, bathing in the veritable cesspit of respiratory particles and bodily fluids sloshing around in the heated atmosphere like a giant Petri dish.

But I switch my doctor brain off and tune in to the beat.

There's a guy up front in ripped jeans and a black T-shirt featuring a white swan with a green mohawk. He's singing about a woman he loves who doesn't know he exists, and the crowd is singing along, hanging on his every word. Lead singer Nester Wild, according to my googling. To one side of him is another guy with an acoustic guitar in skinny jeans that seems like they're painted on his beanpole legs. He's in a plain black tank top and goes by the name West.

The other side of Nester is an Amazon of a woman with bright pink pixie-cut hair, a very short, tiered tartan skirt, ripped fishnets over her solid thighs, chunky boots and a white T-shirt that sits tight against her unfettered A cups and lays bare her navel piercing. She's making the electric guitar hiss and purr like it's followed her right out of band-girlfriend hell. Which is a dumb thought because even though Belle looks like every punk-pixie-dream-girl nightmare and ten times cooler than me on my coolest day, I remind myself that Danny and I are not a thing.

So jealousy is a waste of time and energy.

Unfortunately my brain doesn't give a shit about that as the grungy vibe of hard rock and easy sex pervades everything, and I wonder why in the hell I decided to torture myself like this. I've just come from fifteen hours in the quiet cleanliness of a hospital where everything is hushed and efficient and smells like Glen 20 to this raucous, festering, sexually charged den of rock.

If this doesn't scream two worlds – nothing does.

But then I spot him, and I know exactly why. He's slightly behind the rest of the band, sitting at the drums, belting the hell out of them. His eyes are shut, his head dropped back like he's really riding the beat, and for several moments I forget my insecurities as I feast on the sight of Danny Colton doing what he was clearly made to do.

He's not wearing a shirt, the tats on his chest and abs and neck practically glowing under the pulse of lights, his skin slick with sweat. Sweat sprays from his hair as his head snaps up, the droplets caught by the light. His blue eyes blast open as he leans into a lick and the crowd screams for more.

There's a lot of women, dressed in not a lot considering it's freezing outside – a brisk forty-five. Not in here though. Hence all the skin on display. Bare arms and lots of leg in skirts and short shorts that flash hints of ass cheeks as well as plunging necklines, and skimpy shirts that cover only what needs to be covered.

And that's not just the women.

I'm wearing a skirt that comes to my knee. Also tights and long boots that end halfway up my calves. I took my jacket off as I entered the warmth of the bar and it's hanging over my arm, which leaves me in my form-fitting Henley. It clings to my breasts, the row of buttons that fasten down the middle pulling slightly across my cleavage.

Ordinarily, the V-neck draws attention to my cleavage, and I'd be lying if I said I hadn't thought about that when I'd tossed it in my bag this morning along with the skirt and boots. But as I'm probably the most dressed person here, I doubt anyone's looking.

Damn it... Why did I come?

Because the other night I'd told him I didn't always look like a bridge troll and with another late start tomorrow and him constantly on my mind, I wanted to prove it to him. But I wasn't expecting Danny's world to be so different. This isn't the sparkly world of an arena concert with pyro techniques, backup dancers and big screens that bring the artist closer.

This is the up-close grungy rawness of the bar scene, and I'm intimated in a way I'm pretty sure he was not when he was in my world.

After the other night when Danny had fixed my hot water bottle and massaged my feet, I'd really started to think that maybe he was into me, but now I'm here, I wonder what the hell he sees in me when this is his world.

And he is so in his element here.

I have, literally and figuratively, let my hair down and yet the feeling that I stick out like a sore thumb presses down on me. I should leave but he is mesmerising to watch, and even though I tell myself to get the hell out, I can't pull myself away either. The play of his muscles as he works sticks that are nothing more than a blur makes my nostrils flare.

Or maybe that's the pheromone funk in the air.

But knowing how those muscles have bunched in my palms, how they've flexed over and under and inside me, suspends me in a useless kind of thrall. A thread of something that feels like web silk wraps invisible fingers around my waist and holds me to the spot. I could watch him do this all night.

The drumbeats rise to a crescendo along with the lyrics before they abruptly stop and the crowd breaks into applause. 'Thank you all,' Nester says, his mouth pressed to his mic. 'We're taking a break for a bit but we'll be back. Don't go away.'

The crowd, now released from the clutch of the music, surges forward as the band downs instruments. The raised platform is mobbed by mostly women and in the melee, someone calls Danny's name as he scoops up his shirt, wipes it over his forehead and hair then pulls it over his head. He grins at them as he emerges and gives then a lewd wink, and before I know it I am storming forward, pushing my way through the throng, my pulse an indignant hammer through my head.

*Back off, bitches.*

Music pumps in over the sound system in lieu of the band as Danny's gaze lifts and meets mine. His eyes widen a fraction, but then he slow-grins and even though others are vying for his attention, it's like we're the only two people in the room.

The rest of the band shuffles off stage, but not Danny. He strides purposefully in my direction, stepping off the stage with a single-minded focus that makes me shiver. He's big and hot as he pushes through everyone, staring at me – just me – as he ignores the grab of hands all around him, the sighing, the screaming.

There's an intensity to his gaze which makes my pussy – vagina! – quiver. My heart rate picks up as he bears down on me and I swallow, my mouth as dry as the concrete beneath my feet as he finally reaches me, his hands sliding up my arms.

'Hey,' he says, 'you're here.'

I nod helplessly. I'm breathless, and I don't know what to say. All of my imaginings of him being a drummer in a rock band and it's nothing like I thought it would be. It's... more. He's more. More intense. More raw.

'Why?'

I'm not bothered by his question because I understand why he asks it. This isn't my usual scene and we both know it. I must look like a fish out of water, but... I don't feel it. Not when he looks at me like I belong wherever he is.

'I wanted to prove to you I could rock something other than a duvet and a pair of scrubs,' I say and laugh nervously.

His gaze drifts to my cleavage before drifting back again, appreciation making his eyes glow hot. People all around are trying to get his attention but he ignores them as he says, 'You wanna get out of here?'

I frown. 'Don't you have another set?'

'Not for another twenty minutes.'

He takes my hand then and tugs, and I stick close to him as he drags me through the crowd. I'm super conscious that all these women reaching for him want him – but he's chosen me. I know as they look me up and down, they're wondering why Danny, the drummer/sex god, is with a woman whose knees aren't even visible, and I wonder the same.

How does he want me in this stupid fucking skirt?

Suddenly we're through the crowd then through a door into a long corridor, the noise of the crowd and the interim music instantly muffled. But still Danny doesn't stop; he keeps on striding and I keep on following. We pass an open doorway, and someone calls his name. I turn my head and catch a glimpse of a room where the other band members are hanging, but Danny ignores them, neither turning nor stopping.

I wonder if they know where he's taking me. And why. I also wonder why I don't care.

The corridor gets more dimly lit the further we travel, but I notice the glow of the exit sign ahead and realise we're heading out. When Danny reaches the door, he pushes down on the bar and drags me through to the alley on the other side, the door clunking shut as he gently guides me backwards until my shoulder blades bump into the wall.

It's dark and cool and quiet. The sound of music and the faint smell of garbage are things I'm barely conscious of as Danny smiles and mutters, 'You came.' His hands slide to my hips as his mouth crashes on to mine, hot and urgent, and I open to him and clutch his shoulders, his shirt damp beneath my palms as his tongue licks into my mouth and I breathe him in, filling my senses with the feral sexuality of this sweaty, sexy drumming rock god.

But I want more than just his smell in my head. I want his smell all over me. Like I want my smell all over him. I want to imprint on him so bad. Seeing those women panting after him has really pushed my buttons, and I want to claim him as mine even though I know I cannot compete with that kind of adoration.

My jacket falls off my arm as my trembling fingers slide to the tab of his fly and pop it open. But his hand clamps over mine.

'No,' he mutters as he wrenches his mouth away.

It's gratifying to see him breathing as hard as me, the fog of our combined breath mixing in the cool air between us, but my brain is just as foggy. No? But, why? Why did Danny stop? I am so horny for him right now; even my nipples pressing against the fabric of my bra is too much to bear, and he seemed like he was into it. But he's putting on the brakes and I don't know why.

'Is there something wrong?'

His thumb brushes my bottom lip and it tingles in its wake. 'No. I just... don't want to do this in an alley with you between sets.'

I blink. 'Isn't that why you brought me here?'

'No.' He chuckles. 'I brought you here so I could get you alone. I haven't seen you for a few days and I wanted you all to myself.'

That's good. I know it's good. He wants to see me. And part of me – the scrubs and stethoscope good girl – sings inside. But Danny has woken another side of me and it's wondering *why* he doesn't want to bang one out in the alley with me. I know that's not what I should be hung up on, but I am.

I try not to frown, but I do anyway. 'Why not?'

'Why not what?'

'Why don't you want to do me between sets?'

He chuckles again, his hand hot at my waist. 'Oh, I do. I just... This isn't exactly a hospital, Doc. It's kinda grungy and freezing and there's trash cans not far away and—' He halts abruptly, eyeing me speculatively as he inserts a finger under my chin and tilts my face upwards so he can inspect it thoroughly in the semi dark.

'You want me to fuck you up against this wall in this filthy alley?'

I squirm at the wicked image emblazoned across my inner eye. But Danny seems sceptical. He obviously thinks I need the aroma of antiseptic to get off. Prior to meeting him I might have agreed, but he's making a dirty, dirty girl out of me.

'Isn't that what the women in there want?' I challenge. Those women reaching for him, invading his space like they know how up for dirty-alley sex he really is.

Groupies.

He shrugs. 'Some of them.'

His response depresses me. He knows what they want. If I'd been one of them would we even be talking now? Isn't this what he likes? Isn't this rock and roll?

A small smile tugs at his mouth. 'Jealous, Doc?'

'What do you see in me?' I ask, suddenly serious. 'This world, your world, is so big and bright and colourful and loud and... sexy, and I don't understand why you even want someone as bland and beige as me. There're women back there screaming your name. I'm sure a few would have cut me just now if they'd had a knife to hand.'

Danny regards me through slitted eyes for a second as if he's trying to figure out if I'm for real or not. Then that smile tugs a little bigger. 'You wanna know?' he says, and his voice is low and silky smooth as his hands apply pressure at my waist, and I'm suddenly spun around, cheek and breasts plastered to the cold brick wall.

I gasp at the contact, my palms landing flat above my head for purchase as the move temporarily unbalances me, and then I moan as he pushes in behind me, jamming his hips against mine. My skirt might be sensible and warm but I can still feel the bite of his zipper and the thick ridge of his cock as he presses into me.

'I like that you bashed on my door and weren't reticent in telling me to quit the racket when a lot of dudes I know would have backed the hell away from a six foot four, bare-chested tattooed guy. That's brave. I like that you always hold the door open for old Mrs Appleby. And that you seem to be on call to every resident in the building whether it be a sick toddler or someone's gout playing up. I like that you paid Mr Wong's gas bill last month when he was between jobs. That's kind. You're such a good girl.'

His whispers that like he knows exactly how my body is going to lurch, and I wonder what Mr Wong would think if he could see me in this alley right now.

'I like that you're probably the only woman who's never even attempted to flirt with me, but when it came to the crunch you didn't pretend you didn't want me, you didn't deny the dictates of your desire that night in the elevator. That's decisive.'

His breath is hot at my neck and everything inside me clenches tight as I remember every dirty thing we did the night of the blizzard. A pulse throbs at my temples.

'I like that you're a serious person doing a serious job. I like that you're committed to your studies and have goals. I like that me being a drummer doesn't make you all swoony and giggly because you know that while being in a rock band is awesome, it's not saving the life of a granny or being with someone as they die, and those things are more important. That's smart.'

His voice is as rough as the bricks I am squashed against as he grinds into me to punctuate each point. I can feel the hard outline of his dick as it pushes into the cleft of my buttocks. Another pulse pounds between my legs.

'I like that you came here tonight despite having been at work for God knows how long and your feet are probably aching, but you came looking for me even though your brain can't fathom why it can't resist me. I like that you came anyway. That's hedonistic.'

His hands that had been two hot brands on my hips slide to my breasts, squeezing for a beat or two before his fingers grasp the front of my shirt where the buttons join and rip. I gasp again at the shock of cold brick on my heated flesh and the prickle of the uneven surface taunting the stiff tips of my nipples.

It hurts but in all the right ways.

'That's what I see in you, Doc. I see all the things you are and all the things you want to be if you could just let your hair down and indulge. Like the kind of woman who has sex with drummers in alleys at the back of bars.'

Danny's questing fingers stroke over my bra as he speaks, trailing back and forth along the lacy edge that barely contains their spill. Suddenly he reefs them down, ripping away the fabric protecting my flesh from the hard, freezing surface. My fingers curl into the mortar above my head as I cry out at the shocking cold and roughness that scratches my flesh and abrades my nipples, shooting sensations both painful and erotic straight to my clit.

'Is this what you want, Doc?' He kicks my legs apart and I hold on even tighter as they shake and wobble. 'You want groupie sex?'

I moan, incapable of words as the erotic rub of my nipples edges me closer to orgasm. I want sex in this alley with Danny so damn much it hurts.

'You want me to fuck you? You want me to fuck you in this alley?'

I am an ER doctor; I graduated summa cum lade from med school. I scored 1580 on my SATs. I'm one of only a handful of graduates picked from hundreds of applicants for the prestigious residency programme at the hospital. But I want this drummer to fuck me in this alley more than any other academic accolade I've ever achieved.

He sees me as a whole – doctor and woman – and he has awoken a beast in me.

'Danny, yes, please. Please.'

'Not happening, Doc,' he mutters as his hands ruche up my skirt, cold air swirling around my shaking legs. 'Condom's inside.'

I whimper in protest, but it cuts off abruptly as fingers slide between my legs, find the seam of my tights and rip. I hear the tear even above the jagged chug of our breathing and the drum clash of my pulse through my ears. And then his fingers sweep aside the gusset of my panties and find my slick centre, and my knees almost buckle.

He groans, 'Fuuuuuck, you're wet,' straight into my ear as the grind of his hips keeps me caged against him and the cold brick wall.

His fingers push inside me. One, then two. Another finds my clit. I am a ball of sensation as he grinds against my ass. Cold brick bites at my palms and scrapes at my stiff nipples that I know will be sore for days to come. My nape is stippled in gooseflesh from the hot fan of his breath. My legs tremble. My belly is a mass of contradictions. Taut as a drum on the outside, weird and loopy on the inside.

'Like this, Doc? You like it like this?'

'Yes,' I gasp.

And I do. I don't know what it says about me, but I do. My legs spread, my breasts reefed out of my bra, my tights torn as a guy I've known for a little over a month finger-bangs me hard and rough in a dank, dark, freezing alley. But it works. I am flying.

It takes me no time at all to fly apart.

I moan and thrash, the scrape of brick wall cranking my release as the walls inside me squeeze tight around his fingers and I pant and moan and beg him for more. Beg him not to stop. To never stop.

I am a groupie. Danny has made a groupie out of me.

When I'm done, I can barely hold myself up. I thought my legs were shaking before but it's nothing to the wet-noodle consistency of now. I'm gasping for breath as he withdraws from my body. It's intense. Everything feels so intense. He feels it too, I know.

His breathing is hard and uneven as he presses his face into my nape, his hands grip my hips and his body is heavy against mine as if he too is finding it hard to stand upright. I can feel the rigid length of his still-caged cock in his pants.

There's nothing but two ragged pants for long, long moments, so when the loud bang comes from inside of the exit door, I startle.

'Five minutes, Danny.'

With my heart still racing, I push myself off the wall. He takes a step back, allowing me the space to yank my bra cups up and pull the edges of my Henley together. I can't really do it up as the buttons are mostly gone. I turn, wondering if I look tawdry and dishevelled letting myself be utterly debased in an alley at the back of a bar late on a Saturday night. Or do I look as thoroughly wanton as I feel?

The way his eyes widen then smoulder, I guess it's the latter.

'Are you okay?' he asks, his voice rough.

I nod. My nipples sting and my pussy feels like it's been battered by a ram, but I've never felt better. 'I'm more than okay.'

His lips lift at the sides before he bends over, scoops my coat off the ground and hands it over. I shove my arms in and pull the sides together. I reach for the buttons but he knocks my hand aside and proceeds to do them up instead, his gaze holding mine captive.

'You want to go out tomorrow night?'

I shake my head. 'Working until ten.'

'The next day?'

'A couple of my friends in the residency programme are coming over to study. And then I start a run of seven nights.'

I wasn't exaggerating when I told him I have no time. But my instincts to stay the hell away from Danny Colton are not what they used to be, and I realise I don't want to stay away from him. I want to spend time with Danny. And not just for this. But because he could have dragged any of those women inside out here. Women who are probably all more available and more fun than me. But he didn't.

He chose me.

'But I could break for lunch. We could meet somewhere?'

'Or...' He looks up from the last button and smiles. 'I could drop in and cook pancakes for everyone?'

I meet his eyes at the suggestion, and my breathing, still not quite returned to normal, hitches. Danny in my house. Meeting my friends. Cooking for my friends. That's taking this thing to a whole new level. I hesitate – is that where this is headed? I can try to fool myself as much as I want that Danny and I are about the fucking, but he's cooked for me, massaged my feet, comforted me.

We've talked, gotten to know each other better. There is more to us than just really good fucking. The doctor and the drummer isn't something I ever envisioned with any permanency, but it's not preposterous either.

Is it?

He's seen me at my best and worst. And he's still here. I've seen him surrounded by women all vying for his attention, but he chose me. Maybe it's time I stopped putting up mental blocks between us because I'm worried what other people might think.

'Sure.' I nod. My friends would certainly be up for being fed and meeting the reason why I've been hella distracted these past weeks. 'That would be nice.'

A slow, sexy smile spreads across that addictive mouth. His hand slides onto my jaw and holds me in place as he smashes a deep, hard kiss on my mouth. 'Good answer, Doc,' he mutters as he pulls away. 'Come and meet the band.'

Then he takes my hand and leads me back inside.

# 10

## DANNY

I am incredibly, unbelievably, stupidly nervous as I knock on Holly's door. I have a large container with a just-cooked batch of beef stroganoff in one hand and a shopping bag full of pancake things in the other.

I'm not nervous about cooking. It's who's on the other side of this door that's knotting me up. Who I'm cooking for. Because I'm totally hoping to win over Holly's friends.

Meeting the friends is a big deal. For me. Because I know it's a big deal for her. I'm an easy-going guy and I get along with everyone – seriously, grandmothers love me – but I know Holly's finding it hard to reconcile our two lifestyles. Especially after her impromptu visit to the bar a couple of nights ago.

I hadn't expected her to just turn up, but I'm glad she did. She was clearly a little freaked out by a bunch of women calling my name, but she didn't run away. On the contrary, she'd moved towards me with purpose and determination. And maybe the alley was just a new and liberating experience for her, but it felt more like she was marking me, which was – not going to lie – a real turn on.

Better than that, the band had loved her. Because she'd greeted them like a non-groupie, like they were just normal human beings instead of members of a rock band. Also, they could see how smitten I am.

I don't need their approval but it's nice to have it anyway. And today it's my turn to be put under the microscope and I want the same stamp of approval from her friends.

The door swings open, and it's her. Holly. She's wearing jeans and another long-sleeved Henley with another row of buttons that stretches nicely across her boobs. 'Hey,' she says cheerfully, but I can tell by the dart of her eyes that she's a little nervous too.

I want to kiss her mouth but she's giving off serious *do not invade my body space* vibes as she glances over her shoulder briefly and says, 'Come in.'

It's on the tip of my tongue to whisper *I'm going to rip that shirt open, too* as I pass but I don't because it might throw her off balance and too much is weighing on how this all goes. If her friends don't see us as couple potential then that could be the death knell for whatever fledgling thing we have going on.

Not that I think Holly can't make up her own mind, but I am outside her comfort zone. I am unfamiliar territory. So, of course, she's going to be looking to those she trusts for advice. For, *do-you-think-I'm-crazy?* opinions.

I've been with enough women to know they put a lot of stock in what their friends think, and I want Holly's friends to like me.

'I hope you're hungry,' I announce as I stride into the living area, smiling at Holly's guests. 'I bought enough food to feed an army.'

Placing my cargo on the kitchen counter, I turn to face the two women sitting at the table which is strewn with even more studying debris than the last time I cooked in Holly's kitchen. A black woman with an amazing Afro who is eyeing me speculatively, and a serious-looking redhead with freckles.

Holly is hovering between them like she's temporarily forgotten their names, so I don't wait for introductions. 'Hi,' I say, striding to the first woman and offering my hand. 'I'm Danny.'

She shakes my hand. 'Denise.'

'Nice to meet you,' I say before offering my hand to the redhead, who says, 'Lucy,' as she shakes my hand.

'Nice to meet you, too,' I say.

Denise tips her chin at the counter. 'What you got there?'

'Beef stroganoff. I cooked it an hour ago.'

Cocking an eyebrow at Holly, she says, 'A man who can cook is a good start.'

Hell yes. I am the best start, Denise.

'I'll just pop on some rice and it'll be in your bellies lickety-split.' I know Holly has a rice cooker because I saw it the last time I used the kitchen. And I bought a bag of rice.

I turn back to the kitchen to get started when Lucy says, 'Holly told us we were getting pancakes.'

'You're getting both,' I say as I grab the rice cooker out of the cupboard. 'You need protein as well as carbs while you're studying and I'll mix the batter while the rice cooks.'

I notice the two women exchanging glances in my peripheral vision as Holly says, 'Let me give you a hand.'

Smiling at her, I shake my head. 'No way. Sit. You guys do your thing. Pretend I'm not here.'

Denise laughs. 'You're a man in Holly's kitchen. That's not going to happen.'

Lucy nods in obvious agreement. 'You are the proverbial elephant in the room.'

'Well in that case,' I say, winking at Holly as she sits, 'feel free to talk about me.'

'Oh, we intend to,' Denise claps back.

'Okay, you two,' Holly says good-naturedly, 'back off, let the man work.'

'Hey,' I tease. 'I can multitask.' They laugh as I pour the rice into the cooker. 'So... are you two also in the ER or...'

'I am,' Lucy says. 'Denise is in the surgical residency programme.'

We chat then as the rice cooks and I prepare the pancake batter. About their jobs and where they're from and what their future plans are. They're ambitious and I admire their drive, which reminds me so much of Holly. She doesn't say much, she just sits and listens, but there's this soft smile on her mouth like she's enjoying how well I'm getting on with her friends, and I feel like I'm passing a test with flying colours.

When the rice is done I serve a small amount of stroganoff in ceramic bowls. I don't want to fill them up because the main event is really the pancakes. I'm not exaggerating when I say I make the best pancakes in the entire state and if I haven't won these women over before pancake time, I certainly will after that.

I've not met a woman yet who didn't whimper a little when they took their first ever bite and I don't want these women to be any different. I want them to tell everyone at the hospital about Holly's boyfriend's pancakes.

Because that's what I want to be – Holly's boyfriend. Holly's plus one. Holly's significant other. Holly's ride-or-die.

I want to be Holly's guy.

Sitting here with her friends, laughing and joking and basking in Holly's approval, makes me want it more than I did before I entered the apartment. There is a lot riding on this batch of pancakes.

'So,' Denise says as she blows on a piping-hot spoonful of stroganoff, 'Holly tells us you're in a band.'

I glance up from beating the eggs, meeting Holly's gaze. I wasn't sure what she'd told them about me, but she's obviously shared some info, which is pleasing. The fact she's told them the truth, not tried to obfuscate or embellish, makes me inordinately happy. I guess a part of me feels like I might be a little too low-rent for her and her doctor friends. Or rather that Holly *feels* I'm a little too low-rent.

Okay for a little grungy alley sex but not relationship material.

Neither Denise nor Lucy are peering down their noses at me however, and Holly is looking pretty damn pleased with herself. Like her friends' approval has slotted another piece of the Danny conundrum into place.

'That's right,' I say. 'I'm a drummer.'

They ask me about the band and I answer the usual questions, the small smile playing on Holly's mouth stoking my confidence. I am clearly saying and doing all the right things, charming her friends, and her satisfaction is giddying.

'You got groupies?' Lucy asks as she pushes her finished bowl aside. 'You gotta have groupies.'

'No,' I say.

Holly laughs and bugs her eyes at me. 'Yes.'

My breath catches at the way her eyes dance all happy and flirty like she's not bothered about the women who hang around our gigs because she had marked me in that alley. I smile back. 'Not any more.'

'Ohh.' Denise nods approving at Holly. 'Good answer.'

Holly grins and my breath catches again. She's very different now to the woman who answered the door. That Holly had been worried about how this would unfold. But this Holly is suddenly confident, and hell if that isn't heady AF.

'And that's your plan?' Lucy says. 'For the rest of your life? Playing in a band?'

I want to say something flippant like it's working for Springsteen because I don't think Lucy is being bitchy or judgemental. It seems like a genuinely curious question. But the answer suddenly isn't cut and dried. The truth is I've never thought too far ahead.

But maybe it's time I did?

I take a moment to collect my thoughts as I pour the first lot of batter onto the hot skillet. 'A little while ago if you'd asked me that I'd have said sure.' I glance at Holly, who is watching me intently. 'But now I don't know.'

The truth is being in Holly's orbit has made me reassess my life. She's so driven and goal orientated, which has really shone a spotlight on how aimless my life has been. I don't think that's a bad thing necessarily, I just don't know if it's enough for me any more.

'I'm the kind of guy who takes it one day at a time and I'm lucky that I can earn enough money from doing something that I love to allow me to keep doing it.' I turn my attention to the skillet, idly poking the edges of a pancake. 'But recently I've been thinking about the future and maybe trying new things.'

'Like what?'

I look up at Holly's quick question. I can not only see but feel how invested she is in the answer. Would she prefer me to do something different?

'I don't know. Maybe something that allows me to keep more regular hours.' Not that I think band hours would worry a shift worker. 'And be more protective of my hearing.'

Now I'm being flippant and everyone laughs, but the truth is, hearing loss is a very real occupational hazard in my line of work.

'And maybe,' I add, 'something that has a little more... meaning.'

I think that's what impresses me the most about Holly's job – it means something. That night she told me about the old guy who had died, I knew deep in my bones that she had made a real difference to someone. And that was inspiring.

'Doesn't music bring people meaning?' Denise asks.

'It does.' I nod in agreement as I flip the first pancake. 'But it's often not tangible in anything other than the moment.' Sure, you could listen to our songs on streaming services but that's not like a CD or even a record. 'I think I'd like to be... useful.'

When I fix stuff around the apartment block I feel useful, and that means a lot. It means a lot to Bob and maybe that's him rubbing off on me. Despite what he must have seen, his time in the military hasn't dented his belief in the basic goodness of people.

*Look for the helpers. There will always be helpers.* That's one of Bob's favourite sayings. He stole it from Mr Rogers and used to quote it to me all the time despite the fact the show hadn't been on the TV for two decades.

Maybe I want to be a helper. I hadn't planned on ruminating about my future here today but my thoughts are crystallising just by being in Holly's company. For so long my life has pretty much just been a procession of unplanned days between gigs. Whiling away the hours until the next venue, the next stage, the next crowd. With no real direction other than getting to the end of the gig or the day depending on whether we're playing or not.

Until now. Until meeting Holly. And it doesn't seem enough any more.

Holly is clarifying. I feel like another Danny. Danny Zuko needing to shape up to be Sandy's man.

'You could always do something with food,' Denise muses. 'The stroganoff was to die for and they—' She tips her chin at the griddle. 'Look ah-mazing.'

I grin as I flip the other five bubbling pancakes. 'You wait till you taste them.'

'Who taught you to cook?' Lucy asks.

'Bob,' Holly says.

She smiles at me. I smile back. I like she not only knows this part of my story but jumps in to tell it. There's an intimacy to it and another way of staking her claim.

'The building super?' Denise asks.

I nod. 'He's a relative who took me in for a few years when I was a teenager.'

'What else did he teach you?' Lucy asks.

I smile at all the pearls of wisdom – some more like bombs than pearls – that Bob has taught me over the years. 'He taught me how to mend things,' I tell her. 'From the thermostat in the basement to birds with broken wings. He taught me that punctuality was important because people's time was precious and wasting it was rude. He taught me that if you want to change the world, start by making your bed because how can you accomplish the big things if you don't have time for the small?'

To this day my bed is neatly made each morning.

'He taught me that...' My gaze shifts to Holly and our gazes lock. 'Life is short and if something feels good and right, even if it's only fleeting, grab it with both hands.'

Which was why I joined my first band and went down the path of prioritising my music. Because it's always felt good and right. But now I have Holly, I realise that Bob wasn't talking about things. About possessions. Or jobs.

He'd been talking about people.

I might not be able to fully articulate this feeling I have for Holly, and I'm pretty sure as she holds my gaze that she can't either, but it's important. That I know, for sure.

And the loud bang of my heart concurs.

'He sounds pretty damn wise,' Denise murmurs.

'He is annoyingly so.' I laugh as I drag my gaze off Holly. 'Like a jolly Dalai Lama.'

'Who clearly makes amazing pancakes.' Lucy is practically salivating as she eyes the skillet and, when I put a loaded plate between them ten minutes later, they are like seagulls on a discarded packet of French fries.

The first whimper is Lucy's, and I smile. Still got it. But it's Holly's whimper that grabs at my gut. I want to make her whimper like that for the rest of my life, I realise, and as much as I have enjoyed getting to know her friends, I suddenly wish we were alone so I could watch Holly devour the entire plate just for the joy of listening to that little noise of appreciation and knowing that I'm responsible.

My phone rings as they eat and I check the screen. Smiling, I say, 'Speak of the devil,' and hold up the phone so they can all see Bob's name flashing on the screen.

'Tell him he is a god amongst men,' Denise says around a mouthful of pancake.

I'm laughing as I answer the phone, but it doesn't last long. It's not Bob. It's one of his army buddies – Triton – with bad news. 'What?' I say, not quite believing the words he murmurs into my ear, his voice catching like he doesn't quite believe them either.

Heart attack. Didn't make it.

'What?'

It must be by my tone, or maybe it's just that Holly is as finely attuned to every nuance of my speech and mannerism as I am to hers. She stops eating and frowns just as I seek her out, my eyes fixed on hers. I must look terrible because she stands and says, 'What?'

But I can see in her face she knows what's being told to me on the other end. She's probably had to do exactly the same thing – be the bearer of bad news – so she knows the expression. Denise and Lucy look at me too with the same kind of understanding.

Triton tells me he'll text me some details then I hang up. 'Bob's dead,' I announce, our gazes still locked.

She doesn't say anything, she just crosses the space between us in a flash, her arms sliding around my waist, her head lying on my chest, tucking in under my chin.

'I'm sorry,' she whispers as I lean into her embrace and, knowing she really means it, somehow helps.

\* \* \*

I stare at the beer in the bottom of my glass. It's been ten days since I came to Reno to see to Bob's arrangements, which luckily he had meticulously outlined on his laptop in a folder marked *funeral*. We cremated him today, and tomorrow I will take his ashes back to where Linda is buried not far from the apartment building so he can be next to the woman he loved and adored.

He's eligible to be interred in Arlington, but Linda is buried next to the stillborn baby they'd lost thirty years prior, and Bob's wishes were to be reunited with them in his death.

So that's where I will put him to rest.

But for today, I sit here at his wake surrounded by his ex-military buddies, about a dozen or so grizzled old men, listening to their stories. They're not of war even though many of the stories originate from Desert Storm. They're stories of his sense of humour. Of the practical jokes he loved so much.

They're of Bob'isms.

Of his indefatigable – even back then in the middle of a war – sense that people were good and that even at the end of a gun, kindness and empathy went a long way. That people were people the world over and they wanted the same things.

Peace. Love. Security. Being able to provide for family.

Triton gave the eulogy and quoted the Mr Rogers quote, and everyone nodded and smiled to themselves because we'd all heard it slip from Bob's lips more than once.

As I listen to these men who loved and admired him so much, my own memories play like a movie reel through my brain. Bob teaching me how to fix a flat. Bob insisting that I help him cook in the kitchen every night. Bob assuring me my mother loved me, it was just that some people weren't equipped to be alone.

In so many ways he had provided for me. He'd given me peace, love and security. And I know I'm going to miss his quiet wisdom every day.

I wish Holly was here. I think these guys would like her, especially if she threw in a couple of her own Bob stories. And I miss her. Even giving her space like I have been doing back home these past weeks, just knowing she was in the same building, within easy reach, has been enough. But she feels very far away in Reno.

Too far.

We talk. Text mostly. Between making all the arrangements and commiserating with these guys and her shift work and study, it's easier to drop a message that she can respond to when she gets a moment than making yet another call that goes to her voicemail. Messages can be responded to in those gaps she talks about. Conversations require much more time and, as she was at pains to tell me, she is exceptionally time poor.

But now I'm heading home tomorrow, there's an itch in my blood to see her again. Bob's death has just reiterated some of the things he taught me. Life is fleeting.

Grab it with both hands.

Excusing myself, I pick up my near empty drink and head to the bar, plonking my ass on a stool and indicating through that universal bar sign language that the guy serving should pour another round.

A guy everyone calls Eagle but whose name is actually Ernie takes the stool to my right. He's black and built, with a shock of white hair. He served in Desert Storm with Bob and looks like he could be an enforcer for a biker gang, even in a suit, but it turns out he's a lawyer. He's helped with the arrangements and has been trying to track down Bob's will, which wasn't conveniently on his laptop for easy access.

Triton, who'd disappeared for a while, takes the bar stool on the other side, dropping a large duffel bag on my lap. 'I've been going through the RV and found this stashed under the bed.' Bob always stayed in Triton's decaying old RV parked in his back yard when he came to Reno. 'I'd forgotten about it in the shock of it all.'

The zipper has a thick paper tag attached to it which is yellow from age. 'For Danny Colton' is scribbled on it in black Sharpie.

I stare at it as Triton takes one of the beers the waiter has poured. It's bulky and heavy on my lap as I toy with the tag, the sight of Bob's terrible handwriting taking me back to the notes he'd left scrawled on scraps of paper when some building emergency or other meant he wouldn't be home when I got in from school.

What's in it, I wonder? Something related to his service? Some kind of military go-bag in case of apocalypse? Or something more personal? Something that any of these men would probably be more deserving of?

I unzip the bag and for a moment am confused by the rolls of paper inside. And then I realise. It's... money. A shit ton of money.

Dumbfounded, I pull out a couple of rolls. All ten-dollar bills secured by rubber bands.

I frown at Triton. Then at Eagle. Then back at Triton. 'This is... money.'

'Yup.' Triton chuckles. 'Sure is. That's pretty much all the money he's earned since he's been coming to Reno.'

I blink, not quite able to believe my eyes. The bag is full of it. 'There must be...'

'Couple of hundred thousand,' Triton supplies casually. 'He was a lucky sonofabitch.'

Two hundred thousand dollars? In my lap. 'I don't understand.'

'Bob usually always won big at least once per trip. He'd get it cashed out and chuck it in this bag. For a rainy day. That's what he said.'

If this is supposed to make sense, then it doesn't. 'Why didn't he put it in a savings account?' It wasn't like he was one of those old guys who mistrusted banks.

Triton shrugs. 'I think that was always the plan. He just never got around to it. And then I think he liked the idea of having a stash of cash somewhere. You can take the guy out of the army and all that.'

I think about Bob's modest apartment with its tiny television screen that had been seriously annoying when trying to watch the Superbowl and his old shit box pick-up that he was always tinkering with, fixing one thing or another. He could have bought himself a giant screen, a new car, put a down payment on a house with this kind of cash.

'But he could have used the money.'

'Nah.' Eagle shakes his head. 'I found the will. Trust me, he didn't need it.'

I swing my head in his direction. 'What does that mean?'

'It means Bob had more money than God and you are his sole beneficiary.'

I look at my beer glass and wonder if I'm drunker than I think. Bob has – *had* – more money than God? I find that hard to reconcile with the man I knew who always seemed satisfied with so little.

It doesn't seem possible.

'How much money?' Because richer than God implies extreme wealth. Maybe Eagle was overstating for dramatic effect. Not that he looked like a guy prone to hyperbole.

'With all his investments and extensive share portfolio, he was worth about two billion.'

My brain stops. Literally just goes offline for several beats. Investments? Portfolios?

Billionaire. Bob, who had a TV screen the size of a postage stamp and fixed people's squeaky doors and dripping taps, was a billionaire.

Not a millionaire. A *billionaire*.

'And now you're worth two billion,' Triton adds as if he knows I'm not really taking much in right now and I might need help connecting the dots.

'Yup.' Eagle nods. 'There'll be probate to go through so it might take a while to get everything officially sorted, but... you're a very wealthy man, Danny.'

I blink again. I feel like I've been hit with a stun gun. 'I... don't know what to say.'

Triton slaps me on the back. 'How about you'll pick up the bar tab?'

Eagle snort-laughs and Triton joins in as he holds up his glass. 'To Bob,' he murmurs.

'To Bob,' Eagle repeats, holding his glass up too.

They both look expectantly at me and I make an effort to pull myself together. 'To Bob,' I say, and we tap glasses.

# 11

## HOLLY

It's been almost two weeks since I've seen Danny and I'm stupidly nervous as I approach his apartment door. I don't know why. It's not like it's the elevator all over again. It's not our first time. But he's asked me to stay the night so, in a lot of ways, it feels like the first time.

I've never stayed over. Nor vice versa. Hell, we've not even been on a date – not really. Sure, we've had lunch at my place, but we've not been outside the apartment. And the night I went to the bar where his band was playing hardly counts either. Even if it did come with a happy ending for me.

So spending the night feels... big.

But I want to. I've missed him. And I've worried about him. He's assured me on text a dozen times that he's okay, but I want to see that for myself. To look into his eyes and know it to be true.

If I can know that?

It's at times like this I realise we don't know each other that well, and it scares me. Because how can I feel this... much about a guy I don't know that well?

But I do know the affection and admiration Danny had for Bob. The esteem in which he held him. And the emotional blow he felt at Bob's death, and I do want to be there for him.

He left so abruptly after that phone call, throwing a few things in his car and hitting the road to Reno within a few hours, and I've not seen him since.

Seeing him will be reassuring. And maybe I can be some comfort to him the way he was for me that night after my shitty shift and the period from hell. I want that. Maybe a little too much. Which scares the hell out of me because Danny is making me want more and more and I just don't know how I can juggle it all.

Tonight is a classic example. I was supposed to be knocking on his door over an hour ago, but when three ambulances pulled up outside the ER just as I was about to leave – I didn't. Sure, I could have. I could have been one of those clock-watching, not-my-problem, my-shift's-over sayonara people, but that's not how medicine works.

So, I stayed.

Because that is how it works. That's how being a resident who wants to become an attending works. That's how it is in the ER.

I managed to shoot him a quick text as the first gurney came through the door to alert him, and when I finally got a chance to check my phone as I was leaving, his *I don't care how late you are, just come* is infinitely reassuring, but I can't help but wonder how long until he does care?

How many events do I get to be late to until his patience runs out?

So I'm already arriving on the back foot. Feeling shitty and apologetic as well as nervous. Which is the last thing I want. Tonight should be about him. And the fact I have two days off now does cheer me as I stand in front of his door.

I have to study during the day, but the nights? They're ours. And the thought that I'm going to spend all night in his bed lying next to him sets a little worm of delight squirming through my belly as I wrap my knuckles on the door.

It opens within seconds, and I briefly wonder if he was just standing there looking out the peephole waiting for me to arrive, but then he reaches for me, sliding one arm around my waist and sweeping me inside. I don't get a chance to wonder anything as he pushes the door shut with his other hand and kisses me.

Everything from that second forward is blasted from my brain. I'm conscious of things only on a visceral level. The questing softness of his mouth, the deep probe of his tongue and the faint scratch of his facial scruff that darts an arrow of sensation like heat-seeking missiles straight to my clit. The mint of his toothpaste, the wild musky smell of his cologne, or maybe that's just his pheromones. The hard, unyielding wood beneath my shoulder blades as he pushes me against the door and the loud chug of his breathing.

'Fuck, Doc,' he mutters, his lips brushing mine as his hands slide either side of my face, pushing into my hair. 'I've missed you.'

I can't respond with words as his tongue is back, thrusting eagerly into my mouth, so I moan instead, greeting it with my own as my hands twine around his neck and I clutch him close. His chest is hard against mine and I rub myself against him, trying to ease the tingle in my nipples and the pulse of my clit.

The sensations are everywhere. They are upon me and I pant at how over-whelming they are. I am drowning and he is air.

But suddenly he's pulling away and I am mewing my disappointment. 'I'm sorry,' he murmurs, his hands untangling from my hair and dropping to my hips, his forehead pressing to mine. 'I promised myself I wasn't going to be such a Neanderthal.'

I give a half laugh, breathy and not quite sounding like my own. If he's a caveman than I am a cavewoman because this desire feels utterly primitive. He eases his head back a little so he can look down at me in earnest. 'You've worked all day and you must be exhausted and starving.'

I shake my head. 'I'm fine.' There has been a localised outbreak of gastro this past week and the department has been crazy busy. I've worked back every shift and collapsed into a heap onto my bed after each one, but seeing Danny invigorates me. 'How are you?'

He looks tired. There's a weariness to his eyes that I often see in my own after a long and busy night shift. There are dark smudges beneath too, and his hair looks like it's been stabbed through with his fingers many times over. I know he's pretty much driven straight through from Reno to get home today, but maybe those smudges aren't all to do with fatigue.

'I'm good. All the better for seeing you.' He smiles, slow and warm and like just looking at me is restorative, and I know exactly how he feels, but that wasn't what I meant.

'But how are you – really?'

He nods in acknowledgement. 'I'm okay. Really.'

Another smile. One that reassures. The fact he doesn't say *good* that he says *okay*, is heartening. It acknowledges that it's impossible to be good right now but that he's coping. And I love that he doesn't feel the need to be all stiff-upper-lip over the loss of a person who meant so much in his life.

'You want to eat? I got some pizza delivered earlier. There's a couple of slices left.'

I haven't eaten since I shoved a piece of toast in my mouth about four this afternoon. And I'm bursting with a hundred questions. But I've gone longer without food and the questions can wait. There'll be time for sustenance and communication.

There is a much more pressing need.

I feel it in the eager strain of his body and the answering strain in my own. I can sense it in how he's trying to bank the fever in his blood, the one that is echoed in *my* blood. I can hear it in the husk of his warm breath fanning my face, infecting my own respirations with a roughness that burrs at my throat.

Since the moment I hugged Danny after the phone call and he leaned into me, I've wanted to offer him solace. In whatever form that took. And sometimes solace can be carnal. Sometimes bodies can provide things that food and words cannot.

'I don't want pizza,' I whisper as I use my still-twined arms to tug down on his neck, rising on my tip toes to meet him halfway. 'I only want you.'

When his mouth comes down on me this time, there is no need for restraint and I feel his shudder right down to my bones. The hard vice of his hands clamped on my hips is broken and they move finally, smoothing up my body to my breasts, which they stroke and knead, his fingertips rubbing over my nipples, which burgeon then bead beneath the onslaught and light a fiery path of desire straight to the slickness between my legs.

I moan mindlessly against his lips as a vortex of sensation spirals from my mouth to my nipples to my clit, spreading tentacles of pleasure, digging fiery fingers into my ass and thighs. And I need more. More of him. All of him.

My hands move now, to the haunch of his shoulders and the contours of his back, dragging his T-shirt up and tearing it off his head. His skin is hot and smooth beneath my palms as they explore lower, sliding to the tight bunch of his ass, which I squeeze with as much fervour as he's kneading my breasts.

His groan is satisfying in ways I never knew existed.

He grinds against me and I gasp as I hook a leg behind his thigh to give him better access, which he ruthlessly exploits but I still need more. The thump of my pulse, the tremble of my hands, that fever in my blood almost at boiling point now, demands more. I want to feel the hard steel of his cock in my palms and thrusting deep inside me.

His absence has unbalanced me in ways I didn't realise until I saw him just now and I want to ground myself in him. Feel his possession.

I want to feel... completed. I want him to feel completed, too.

My hand slides to his waist, to the button of his jeans, fingers fumbling as they reef it open and pull down the tab of the zip. They slip beneath the band of his underwear and wrap around his solid girth, and my whole body sighs at the feel of it.

This. Mine. Danny.

He cries out, his mouth tearing away, pressing into the side of my neck, his whiskers prickling deliciously at my skin. I fist him, stroking from the root to the tip, and he groans so gutturally I feel it as a rumble through the earth beneath my feet.

It's subterranean. A fault line quivering.

As if the intimate clutch of my hand has broken the seal, Danny is no longer content to squeeze and stroke. With his lips a brand at my neck, he plucks at my shirt, pulling it up and off, his fingers immediately reefing down the cups of my bra before making short work of the back clasp.

His lips move south, his scruff an erotic scrape, his mouth hot as he sucks on an achingly stiff nipple. I gasp, spearing the fingers of my spare hand into his nape. His teeth graze the sensitive tip and it sparks like an electric shock. I moan as it ripples across my flesh, his mouth transferring to the other side, hands moving relentlessly down, finding the waistband of my very sensible work trousers and making short work of the fastenings.

'Off,' he mutters around my nipple, hot hair puffing on the wet aureole as his hands peel both trousers and underwear down to my thighs.

I take over as his fingers return to more interesting tasks, wriggling out of the fabric and my shoes as they taunt the aching tightness of a nipple and slide between my legs. I buck and moan his name as he so deftly finds my clit. 'Danny.'

His breathing is heavy as he groans in response. 'Fuuuuck. You're so wet,' he mumbles into my neck. 'Need you.'

Need. That word is like an accelerant to the passion blazing between us. That Danny wants me has never been in dispute. That he needs me? That's a whole other ballgame. It implies lack of control. Something that cannot be explained or contained – it just is.

'Condom,' I pant as I double fist his cock, my thumbs smearing the liquid beading from the slit over the taut flushed dome of his head. I need him too, despite all the reasons why I shouldn't that percolate through my brain on the regular. I need him more than oxygen. I need him more than any bodily sustenance.

I need him beyond reason.

So much so I am fully naked again while he is mostly still clothed and guiding his cock towards my centre, greedy, even without the requested condom.

Thankfully, though, the mention of protection – or maybe something else – has roused him from our thrall and he pulls back, the harsh sound of our combined laboured breathing the only noise in the entire apartment.

His gaze rakes over me. My hair half out of its confines from the thrust of his fingers, my mouth swollen from his kisses, my nipples wet and taut from his attention, my hands circling his cock that is jammed between us.

'Fuck.' He shakes his head, his voice full of gravel. 'I think I must be a Neanderthal because the way I've marked you makes me want to beat my chest.'

I glance down to see the abraded areas of skin on my chest and around my nipples where his whiskers have scratched me up, and hell if I don't want to roll my back and preen under his approval. I suppose I should reject the entire notion of being marked by a man, but the streak of possession in his tone has me going full cavewoman.

'So why are you stopping?' I ask as my gaze drops to my hands.

He follows, and I perform a slow, deliberate up and down as he watches, his eyelids fluttering closed briefly as I complete the manoeuvre before they open again. 'I want to show you something first.'

He kisses me hard and quick as his palms slide over my ass to grasp the underside as he lifts me up like I weigh nothing at all. His hands are firm under the tops of my thighs, my legs automatically parting to grip either side of his hips, his cock perilously close to my entrance as it slides along my folds.

'Hold on tight,' he whispers into my ear.

I squeak a little as he takes off, my hands clutching around his neck as he strides through his apartment. Laughing at his skill, he cuts me off with his mouth and I moan and cling even more as he walks blindly on, his lips plundering mine, navigating the landmarks of his space without bumping into a single one.

The thickness of his erection is an erotic tease with every footfall, and I squirm against him to increase the delicious friction until he finally draws to a halt. My eyes flutter open as he pulls out of the kiss. His slumberous gaze locks on mine, his mouth wet, and my internal muscles turn to warm jello as he looks at me with frank possession.

With a smile, he eases his hands away and slowly lowers me. I shiver as his cock slips between my folds, teasing my hard, swollen clit, then drags along my belly before my feet hit the floor, which crinkles a little underfoot. There's something odd about that, but pleasure ripples through the muscles slung between my hips and then the mattress hits me behind the knees, so I don't pay it any heed.

He flattens his palm against my chest. 'Timber,' he murmurs, blue eyes dancing.

I smile as he increases the pressure gently on my sternum. Playing along, I fall back against the mattress. Which also... crinkles. Like the duvet is made of wrinkled paper. Taken out of the moment, I glance either side of me. A bedside lamp throws some light across the cover, and I frown.

Is that... money?

I look at Danny, who is standing there grinning at me now, his arms crossed, which only emphasises his incredible biceps and the art that decorates them. Levering myself up onto my elbows, I twist my head from side to side again, taking in the entire mattress this time.

It is money. Ten-dollar bills to be precise.

The mattress is covered in a thick layer of money and as I watch, one slides off to the floor. Absently scooping up a handful, I stare at it. Fake, I'm assuming. I mean, they look real, but I see enough news to know that fake money can look genuine, and there's no way this could be real because there must be thousands of them.

I blink, confused. What the hell is going on? Why on earth is there fake money strewn across Danny's bed? I let the handful drop to the mattress as I look to him for answers.

'Is this some kind of kink you wanted to show me? I mean, if role-playing that you're some kind of millionaire that likes to fuck on a pile of fake money is what floats your boat then I can get on board with that.'

I'm sure there are weirder kinks out there. But then, what would I know?

The most risqué sex thing I've ever done was letting a guy I barely knew debauch me in a broken-down elevator. Pretty vanilla really.

'No.' He shakes his head and laughs. 'Not a kink and not fake. One hundred per cent genuine.'

I frown. 'It's real?'

'Every single note.'

Sitting properly, I pluck up the nearest bill and hold it towards the light. Not that I have any clue what I'm looking for. I glance at Danny again. 'There must be thousands here.'

He nods. 'About twenty thousand ten-dollar bills. And they're all mine.'

I do a quick calculation in my head. That's... two hundred thousand dollars. What the hell? 'Did you do some gambling while you were in Reno? Or...' The note I'm holding falls from my fingers to the floor. 'Rob a bank?'

'None of the above. That lot is a stash of Bob's casino wins over the last decade. And it turns out he has much, much, much more than that in the bank and in a truly mind-blowing investment portfolio.'

I'm waiting for Danny to tell me he's joking, but I can see he's not. 'Is he like some kind of... secret millionaire?'

He shakes his head slowly. 'More than that.'

More? Is Danny saying... 'He's a billionaire?'

'Yep.' He grins. 'And I am his sole beneficiary.'

I stare at him, not quite believing the turn of events. 'Oh my God.'

'Yup.'

'Oh my God,' I repeat.

He laughs as he repeats, 'Yup.'

I glance around me and scoop up armfuls of ten-dollar bills and let them fall. They're cool against my naked flesh, some landing in my lap while others skim my body.

'So...' I drag my eyes off the river of cash to meet his. 'You're rich now?'

Danny lets out a long breath that fluffs the hair hanging over his forehead. 'Apparently.'

'What are you' – I look around, completely flummoxed – 'going to do with it all?'

My mind is crowding with a hundred different questions, but none of them can get past the glitch going on in my brain.

Danny is rich. Danny is rich. Danny is rich.

He's not this blue-collar guy with tats and swagger, at home in jeans and a tool belt and sitting behind a drum kit. Not any more. Now he is seriously fucking rich. I don't know what that means. It's just too damn big to even wrap my head around.

'I don't know yet,' he says. 'But I do know what I want to do with it tonight.'

His eyes have gone hot again as his gaze lands on the ten-dollar notes that are decorating my thighs. I swallow at that look that reminds me I am completely naked and his dick is out and still hard and flushed and lethal. His eyes trek up my body slowly until they finally meet mine.

'Ever fucked a billionaire?' he asks, the corners of his mouth lifting.

I laugh. 'Nope.'

'Ever screwed on top of two hundred grand?'

My smiles gets bigger. The whole notion is so damn absurd. Also thoroughly, utterly debauched. 'Nope.'

'Well, then.' Fishing in his back pocket, he pulls out a silver foil packet before stripping out of jeans and underwear and kicking them aside. 'This is your lucky night.'

He's right. It is my lucky night. And not just because I am lying on a literal bed of money but because this is the first time I've seen him completely naked, and he does not disappoint. My mouth goes as dry as those ten-dollar notes as I trace the twine of inky vines that wrap around his legs from his ankle to the bulk of his quads.

And further north to narrow hips and the ladder of his abs and the span and breadth of his chest and shoulders decorated in a breastplate of ink. Unfettered by clothes, Danny's body could have been Da Vinci's inspiration for *Vitruvian Man*.

He advances on me then and I fall back onto my elbows and watch him, the gleam in his eyes purely carnal. Pausing at my knees, he holds my gaze as he tears the foil packet open and rolls the condom down his shaft. He shudders at his own touch and I feel an answering shudder as the walls of my vagina squeeze tight in anticipation.

'Spread your legs,' he says, his eyes still on mine.

I can smell my arousal as I slowly comply, easing onto my back as I do so, money crinkling and sticking beneath me. He looms over me, placing one hand near my head while the other scoops up a bunch of notes, which he lets fall all over my body. He does it again until my torso is strewn with ten-dollar bills.

Only then does he drag his gaze off mine to admire his handiwork. Bills pile on my belly, cover my mons and my nipples, slide off the slopes of my breasts and the cage of my ribs. I am conscious of the crinkle of cash as I flatten my palms into the duvet.

'Fuck, that looks good on you,' he mutters.

My breath catches at the reverence in his voice, but I need more than his eyes on me. More than his money on me. I need him on me. Covering me. In me.

'You know what else looks good on me?' I say, my voice husky. 'You.'

I reach for him them and drag him down, moaning as his weight presses me into the mattress and his pelvis settles against mine. My legs, ten-dollar bills sticking to my inner thighs, wrap around his waist and I feel the thick nudge of him butting my slick entrance.

'Now,' I whisper in his ear. 'Please.' It's been too long since he's been inside me, and never like this.

Never horizontal. Never nose to nose. Never skin on skin. This is intimate. It's not the furtiveness of a hospital closet. It's not the riskiness of a broken-down elevator or the public thrill of a grungy alley.

It's just us, alone – no risk of being caught or interrupted. It's the stuff of lovers.

He kisses me as he drives his cock inside, swallowing my moan and his groan as they erupt from a place inside that seems to be shared. I open to him. My mouth to his kisses, my centre to the thrusts of his cock, and I'm exactly where I want to be.

It doesn't take long. Not for either of us. It's too much this first time – this first proper time. It's been building for too long. We find our peak quickly and let go together, my hands scooping up piles of ten-dollar bills, letting them rain down around us as we gasp and groan and shudder through an intensity of pleasure and passion.

## 12

### DANNY

I don't know how many times we make love. Yes – make love. It doesn't feel like fucking. Like something recreational and unimportant. It feels hella important. Like there's an added layer beyond the physical that deepens our frantic joinings.

We roll around in the money all night until, much like cookie crumbs in the bed, it ends up everywhere. Not that we care. We just doze off for a bit and wake again for more.

We are insatiable.

It's not that we don't have plenty to say – we both know there's a lot to talk about – it's more that this is the first time we've had such continuous access to each other and neither of us wants to squander the opportunity. She's not on shift or studying. I'm not at a gig or hundreds of miles away in Reno.

Those pesky things that have kept us from each other don't have any place between us tonight, and knowing I can just put my hand out and feel her next to me is a reassurance I never knew I was missing.

I think maybe she feels the same way. Because there's an intensity to how she kisses me, touches me, looks into my eyes. As if she's trying to convey solidarity with her body. Trying to convey that although life is full and fast and busy, she's here for me. I know it's what I'm trying to convey with mine.

Amongst other things.

There's a lot of miles between here and Reno, and all that quiet time helped crystallise my thoughts. This thing between us has been unexpected. And a whirlwind. But not, at least for me, unsurprising. I knew there was something different about Holly from the start. Stupidly, or maybe cockily, I thought it was her shyness, her coyness. The way she avoided my gaze. Avoided me.

Not something women usually do.

But it didn't take me long to realise it wasn't that she was different to other women – because she's not. It's the way I feel about her that's different.

As much as I sing a bunch of songs that talk about love at first sight, I've never been a true believer. Until Holly. Because the truth is I don't just want to be her boyfriend and see how things go – I'm falling in love with her. And if I didn't know before I went away to Reno, I know it now.

And I think she feels the same way. I think that's what she'd been trying to say with her body all night long even if her brain isn't quite there yet.

The clock tells me it's twelve minutes past ten when my eyes finally open, which is not surprising considering how very little sleep we snatched in between the sexy times. The room is quiet apart from the soft cant of Holly's breathing. She is lying on her stomach, her head turned away from me, her dark hair spread across her shoulder blades having come loose from her pony-tail many hours ago.

The sheet is half pulled up, covering one soft, rounded ass cheek only. The other one is as exposed as the rest of her, that leg twisted in the sheet, tugging it down, and I give my eyes free reign to rove and wander. Over the dimples just above her ass, down the slope that forms the dip of her back, up the other side to the notches of her spine and the flare of her ribs to the steady rise and fall of her chest.

Her skin is white. Unmarked by tan lines or tattoos. But it is the perfect canvas and I can imagine it all inked up, a piece of art so intricate and fasci-nating I'll never be able to get enough of looking at it. What would she choose, I wonder? To decorate her skin?

She's not a skulls and crossbones kinda woman. No anarchy tattoos for Holly. Flowers, I reckon. Or maybe something medical related. Something a little nerdy.

There's a ten-dollar note stuck to her upper arm and my smile broadens.

Most of the money is on the floor now having been pushed off as we greedily used the entire mattress surface for our sexual shenanigans, thrashing our way through multiple orgasms each. But I can still see a bill here and there as I gently peel the one off her arm and toss it over the side.

It's going to be much harder to collect and roll and bag the notes than it had been to free them from their rubber-band confinements and let them flutter over the bed.

Holly stirs, lifts her head, looks over her shoulder. She pushes her hair off her face as her gaze meets mine. 'Good morning,' she murmurs, her cheeks pinking up.

I grin. 'Good morning.'

How she can blush after the debauchery of the lift and the frequency and intensity of last night, I have no idea. But I love that this thing between us is still new enough for her to feel that coyness. And also that she's not casual or flippant about sex.

I've been too casual and flippant about it throughout my life and suddenly wish that last night had been my first time. That it had been Holly who had popped my cherry, not my junior prom date when I was fifteen.

'What time is it?' she asks as she rolls onto her back.

I laugh as she reveals two more notes stuck to her torso and a scattering of faint red marks from my whiskers. I should be mortified by them but perversely, I like seeing them in the morning light and knowing that she got them from me.

'Just after ten,' I tell her as I lean in and remove them with my teeth and linger for a while, nuzzling slowly north, my nose brushing her nipples as I skate higher still, intoxicated by the smell of sex and money on her skin.

'Hmm.' She shuts her eyes on a sigh of pleasure. 'I wish I didn't have to study today.'

'So don't.' I lean in to nuzzle the side of her neck. 'Play hooky for a day,' I whisper in her ear.

She gives a half laugh as I prop my head on my hand to watch her face. Her eyes blink open as she says, 'Get behind me, Satan.'

I grin wolfishly. 'I can do you from behind.'

Just then her stomach, or maybe it's mine, growls loud enough to bring the fucking ceiling down. We look at each other for a moment then burst into laughter. My bent elbow collapses and I face-plant into the crook of my neck where my laughter muffles.

'I'm being a terrible host,' I say as I raise myself again so I can look into her face. Her lips are kiss swollen and that, too, pleases me. 'You're obviously starving.'

She slides a hand to her belly which I track. 'I could eat,' she admits. 'But I'm not about to fade away.' Her fingers rest low and while part of me wants to see them go further, delve between her legs and watch as she gives herself a little morning glory, the fever from last night has been turned to a low simmer for now so, when she raises her hand to my jaw, I drag my gaze back to her face.

'Talk to me,' she says. 'Tell me about Reno.'

My eyebrow quirks. 'About Bob? Or the money?'

She smiles as her index finger brushes my temple. 'Bob first. Money after.'

I ease back onto the pillow, my mind crowding with all the things I want to tell her about the last couple of weeks. I'd always known Bob was a good guy but nobody, it seemed, had a bad word to say about him, and to see the level of respect and admiration from his military buddies was something really special. Then there were the stories about how many lives he'd touched just through his good works.

So many from so many different people I don't even know where to start. So I tell Holly all of them. And she listens attentively, her head on my shoulder, her thigh slung over mine, her arm across my chest, her fingers drawing little circles on my shoulder as I speak. She interjects every now and then with an observation or a comment, sometimes a laugh, but otherwise she just listens and pets me, and I know this is what I want going forward.

Her and me together like this, our lives intertwining.

When I eventually run dry, she doesn't say anything for a long time. We just lay there, content in our embrace. Eventually she rouses, using her clenched fist on my chest to prop her chin and look at me. 'What are you going to do with all this money?'

'I don't know. What do you think we should do with it?'

She gives a half laugh. 'We?'

'Sure. You and me.' If Holly's going to be part of my life, of course I want her to help me spend it. 'There's so much good we can do, but we can also do a bunch of stuff that's completely and utterly wild, right?'

Her brow crinkles a little, although she is still smiling. 'Well, sure... that sounds great... but I've not got a lot of spare time the next five years.'

'Holly.' I laugh then. I love how dedicated she is that she can't even see how much this potentially frees her up. 'Don't you see? You don't have to worry about any of that any more. Your days of being constantly exhausted and stressed at how little time you have for an actual life are over. You don't have to work. Or study. You certainly don't have to worry about not being quick enough to dodge an incoming smack.'

A lock of her hair falls forward and I absently twist it around my finger as I speak.

'You'll have the kind of financial freedom most people only ever dream of. You can do whatever you want whenever you want. You can go buy a house. Hell, you can buy multiple houses. You can travel any time you want. You can buy art and jewellery and go to all the best shows. You can sit at Centre Court at a Wimbledon grand final or track-side at a Grand Prix and eat out at the best restaurants.'

Okay, yes, I'm getting a little carried away. I have no idea if Holly is in to any of those things, but that's not the point. None of these would have been possible in my wildest dreams prior to this surprise inheritance. I've not ever coveted a wealthy existence, but to be able to give one to the woman I'm falling for? The only woman I've ever fallen for?

I'm giddy with the possibilities.

'Hell, we can just hop from one beach resort to the next. Get matching tans and tattoos and when we get older, some his and hers matching plastic surgery to keep us looking as young as we're going to feel with all that money at our disposal.'

The more suggestions I rattle off the quicker Holly's smile fades. By the time I run out of fanciful ideas, she's actually frowning. She doesn't say anything for a beat or two, but there is a lot of blinking going on.

'Okay,' she says eventually as she pushes away from me, sliding to the side of the mattress, her feet landing on the floor. Rising from the bed, she drags the sheet with her, wrapping it around her body as she looks over her shoulder at me. 'I think you need to take a breath, Danny.'

Her voice is quiet but serious and I realise as she tucks the sheet to secure it at her cleavage that I've gone too far. 'Okay... sorry.' I give a deprecating laugh as I haul myself into a sitting position, my back to the wall behind. 'I'm getting ahead of myself.'

'You think?'

Her laugh holds an edge of hysteria as she takes several paces away from the bed, the sheet trailing behind like a bridal train, sweeping through a carpet of Alexander Hamiltons.

'I've freaked you out, haven't I?'

Damn it, I really should have kept my wits about me. Holly has always been on the skittish side without me going off half-cocked high on a life-changing inheritance and the delirium of scant sleep thanks to a killer drive followed by a night of serious dick.

'You could say that.'

'I know. I'm sorry. I'm just trying to say… very ineptly that… I love you and I want us to be together and I'm excited for our future.'

If I thought that might help, it didn't. Holly pales as she says, 'Oh God…'

Suddenly she looks like she's going to have one of those old-fashioned fainting spells as she clutches the sheet tighter. Christ, I'm fucking this up, big time. Leaping from the bed, I scrabble around for my underwear. I locate my jeans and snatch them up, more tens fluttering to the floor as I strip my under-wear from inside them and step into them.

'You love me?'

Yeah… she's freaked out. But I'm not going to pretend I don't. It might not be the way I intended on telling her but I'm not about to deny it either.

I shove my hands on my hips. 'Yes.'

'Danny…' She shakes her head at me. 'This is… grief and a huge life-changing thing that's happened to you. It's… discombobulating.'

'No.' I shake my head at her. 'It is those things, yes. But that doesn't mean it isn't also love.'

I know I just dropped it this on her – but the longer it's out there the more I'm certain of it, and she might not believe it – which is fair – but I need her to know that I believe it. That I'm not screwing around with how I feel.

Still, she frowns like it's the most preposterous thing she'd heard. 'Okay, so… what happens when this… grand love doesn't last?'

Her dismissive emphasis tells me all I need to know about her feelings on that topic, but *grand love* is the perfect descriptor.

'When down the track we're done and your lawyers screw me out of every last cent you've so magnificently bestowed on me, and I've given up my career and have nothing to fall back on?'

My brain instantly and vigorously rejects this scenario. 'I would never do that.'

Holly glares at me and I realise, in my rush to assure her I would never be so malevolent, that I've missed the point.

'What makes you think I would give up my dream of being a doctor because my...'

I hold my breath, pretty sure she's about to say *boyfriend.* But she doesn't. She pauses as if she's trying to find another adjective to describe who I am to her. 'The guy I'm fucking,' she corrects, 'is suddenly rich?'

Okay, she's truly pissed now. Holly doesn't use the F word that often. Sure, she's using it deliberately to cheapen what's going on between us, but I'd be stupid not to acknowledge the anger behind her words.

And that's on me for how I've handled this.

'No.' I shake my head, tackling the first part of her statement instead. 'You don't have to give up being—'

Her snort cuts me off. 'Gee, thanks.'

'No... I don't mean... Of course you don't have to stop being a doctor, I just know how...'

I falter and she folds her arms. 'How what?' she demands.

'How stretched you always feel. You don't ever seem like you... enjoy it. It seems... hard.'

'Just because it's hard, doesn't mean it isn't worthy.'

'Of course it's worthy.' Is there anything more worthy? 'But... do you enjoy it?'

I love being a drummer, sitting on my stool, picking up my sticks, striking the tom. Feeling the thud against my chest and the reverb that vibrates through every cell in my body.

It's exhilarating. Holly never seems exhilarated.

'I love being a doctor. Yes, it's hard and yes, it's exhausting and yes, I feel stretched pretty thin a lot of the time. And no, I don't enjoy it a lot of the time. But that's just the kind of job it is when you're dealing with people who are sick and scared and worried. It's not always going to be roses and candy canes. But you know why I want to do this, Danny. Why I need to. I told you why.'

I nod slowly. Her grandmother; I remember.

'And I don't want a tattoo, Danny. I don't care if people do and yours look amazing, but it's not for me.'

'Jesus, Holly.' I shove a hand through my hair. 'I don't care about that.'

'I know,' she says, shaking her head. 'But it's not just about that. I don't need diamonds or the best concert tickets or a mansion to live in. Neither apparently did Bob. I want to be a rural ER specialist with all the triumphs and yes, the stress that comes with it.'

'But you can do so much more than that with our money,' I say. 'We'll have enough to buy every rural hospital in the country the best people and equipment available.'

Sure, I've just reeled that off the top of my head but... why not? It's as good a cause as any, right?

She seems momentarily lost for words before she says, 'Okay, sure. That's an option. But... I want to work, Danny. I want to be at the coalface. I'm sure there are plenty of women out there who'd love to swan around the world, and there's nothing wrong with that. In fact, I think you should go and find one of them because I don't think I'm the right person for you.'

I blink at the statement. Like she's interchangeable, this woman I love.

'I don't want anybody else,' I snap, stung that she thinks I'm that shallow. That what I feel for her is that frivolous. How has this derailed so quickly? 'Maybe I don't know what I'm going to do with this money and how it's going to impact my life. Maybe I don't have all the answers yet, but I do know I want you in my life.'

She sighs a little. 'Look, Danny... all of this has thrown you for a bit of a loop. That's fair enough – becoming an overnight billionaire is big. So maybe what you need more than anything else is to figure out what it's going to mean for you and your life before you start involving others. With that much money you need to be considered and certain, not reckless.'

I huff out an aggrieved breath. I hate how she sounds so reasonable and I want to reject the advice, but it's good – sensible. The type of advice that comes from a woman who has a life plan, who doesn't live from day to day, gig to gig.

Who I love.

And maybe the best way to show that is to offer her a future with a guy who has a plan that's solid, not half-baked. A plan for me – not her. But one that allows her to slot in if and where she feels comfortable.

'Is this the polite doctor way to tell me I need to sort my shit out?'

She laughs. 'I guess, yes.'

Her laugh eases the tension in my chest. She's not looking at me like some kind of monster any more that let a bunch of money go to his head and suddenly morphed into some ridiculous parody of a sugar daddy.

'You told Denise and Lucy that you wanted to do something with meaning. This money surely gives you the opportunity to something really meaningful. For you. And Bob. Not for me.'

That's right – I had said that. I guess with everything that happened straight after that, it went by the wayside. 'That could take a while.' Especially considering I don't even know where to start.

She shrugs. 'I'm not going anywhere.'

The confirmation floods me with relief. I didn't totally blow it then. There's still hope. Once I've sorted my shit out. She's giving me a chance to retreat and rethink. 'But what will you do without my wonder schlong in your life?'

One of my bad habits is to try and lighten tense situations with humour. A lot of the time it doesn't work. Thankfully, Holly laughs. 'I'm sure I'll survive.'

Survive. I frown at the desolation of that term. 'That sounds bleak.' I say it with a faux dramatic shudder to soften the words. But the thought of Holly surviving, just going through the motions of her life like before she met me, makes me want to peel my skin off.

'I'll...' She shrugs. 'Finally get that vibrator.'

Part of me is insulted that she thinks a silicone dick is a worthy substitute, but the fact she still doesn't own one is depressing. 'Yes, but will you, is the question?'

Because I know her, now. She'll fall back into her old ways of neglecting her sexuality and although I don't plan to stay away for too long, she should still be loving herself on the regular.

She rolls her eyes. 'Yes.'

'Really?'

She bugs her eyes this time. 'Yes.'

She smiles then and I smile back, and I love her so much it hurts. The heat has gone out of our argument but the end result is still the same – she's going to walk away. As if reading my mind, she gives a little shrug. 'I'd better get going.'

I want to ask her to stay a bit longer, but she has to study and I have some serious research to do, too. So, I just nod and say, 'I'll call tomorrow.'

'Okay.' She sweeps out of my room then like a runaway bride, the sheet trailing behind as she heads for where her clothes were discarded last night. There's a catch in my chest. A pain. Sharp and stabby. More painful than I even imagined watching her leave.

Way to fuck things up, dufus.

# 13

HOLLY

Two weeks. It's been two weeks. Normally the weeks fly by thanks to shift work and study and the never-ending treadmill of exhaustion, but these two weeks have moved slow as molasses. And nowhere near as sweet.

Danny loves me.

Danny loves me.

Danny loves me.

I'm supposed to be studying. There are papers and open textbooks strewn across the table. But all I can think is Danny loves me. I panicked when he blurted it out because it instantly felt like a jigsaw piece clicking into place, but how could that be?

Yes, there were feelings, but... love?

It seemed too soon and too quick and too... half baked. Too like Danny and not enough like me with my bullet journal and ten-year plans, erupting from the middle of his stream of consciousness trip into fantasy land about living like the Kardashians.

I suppose a lot of women would be thrilled if the guy they were... seeing suddenly came into lots of money, but my parents worked too hard put me through college and I've worked too hard to get where I am just to throw it all away to become a lady of leisure. Forget the reason why I became a doctor in the first place.

Although, I admit as I stare at the books in front of me, bleary-eyed, some days that has a certain amount of appeal.

I know he was excited and letting himself wax lyrical, but I've been grappling all along with the dichotomy of us. Future ER-attending Holly rejecting the idea of letting myself feel anything for a drummer in a rock band who doesn't think past his next gig versus elevator/alley Holly feeling all the feels. So his smorgasbord of decadence seemed the classic representation of our differences. He seemed so like my ex, Warren-like in that moment, expecting me to fit in with his plans, and everything just slowly froze inside me as my brain blared *back away!*

*Back the hell away.*

Even if it has been, ever since, thinking – very unhelpfully – overtime about him and how his declaration of love has seeped into all my nooks and crannies and the ways I could help Danny spend his money. The good he could do with it.

*We* could do with it.

But he needs to figure that out himself. He needs a plan for it – that part was at least the truth. Money like that is a big responsibility. If a person wanted to do something meaningful with their life, anyway.

A sudden knock on my door yanks me out of the cyclical trap of my thoughts. My pulse spikes. Danny? Could it be him? He's stayed away, as have I because that's only fair after insisting he sort his shit out. But that doesn't mean it's been easy.

It doesn't mean my body hasn't craved his in the middle of the night. Or my finger hasn't hovered over his number in my phone just so I could hear his voice again or tell him about the latest entry to the ER ass box.

Shaky legs take me to the door, but it's not Danny, and for a moment I just stare at the UPS guy, who greets me with a friendly smile and holds out a rectangular parcel. It's from Amazon. I take it automatically, even though I know I haven't ordered anything from them.

Like I get time for online shopping.

But it has my name and address on the front. Maybe my mom ordered something for me and forgot to say anything?

I sign for it, and he leaves, and there's just me and the parcel. I should put it aside for later, but it's not like I'm being particularly productive right now.

Thinking about Danny and how much I miss him instead of ventilation proto-cols for inhalation burns is not getting me anywhere.

I sit and tear open the parcel to reveal a box with a picture of a bright pink dildo on all four sides. And the lid. I blink, momentarily stunned. My mom sure as hell hasn't sent me this. Which only leaves one person. I look through the discarded packaging and find the note.

Because I know you haven't gotten around to it yet...
    Love Danny xxx

I blink again at his choice of words. *Love Danny*. My heart gives a funny little double beat as those two words stare back at me. A standard, familiar way to sign off a card, sure, but also a reflection of his true feelings.

Even if I hadn't wanted to hear them.

The thought gets me so churned up, I actually transfer my attention back to the box. Gingerly, I open the lid, like I'm afraid it might leap out and insert itself in my vagina of its own accord. It doesn't, so I upend the box, and the packaged dildo falls into my lap.

Tentatively, I pick it up. The crinkle of the clear plastic is loud in the silent room. It's long and thick and hard, cylindrical rather than being any kind of life-like representation of the male anatomy, and I'm back in the elevator with Danny and the screwdriver.

My body responds in kind. My nipples ache as if they're being pinched, and my pelvic floor contracts in some kind of wild Pavlovian muscle memory. A warm slipperiness slicks my folds as I rip it out of its plastic, needing to ease the roar inside me so damn bad, I don't care how I achieve it.

And it's a lot safer than calling Danny.

A strong waft of plastic wrinkles my nose. The latex aroma is almost over-whelming, and I thank God I'm not allergic. I'd probably already be rolling on the floor with my airway closing off just from the smell alone.

Danny doesn't smell like that.

I think about the real thing, and my urgency dies. It's not the same. It doesn't look the same or feel the same. It sure as hell doesn't smell the same. It's not the real thing, and that's suddenly what I need. Not just *anything*.

I need Danny.

And not only for what he's packing inside his underwear and his willingness to put it at my service, but because he's the first man ever who's made me think about anything other than my job. Because he's made me believe I can actually have a life outside medicine.

Because he's likes having sex with me but he wants more than that, too.

He's offering me a life, and for the first time, looking at this godawful dildo, I actually want one. Because he's been dogged and determined in his pursuit of me, despite my lack of encouragement. Because his smile turns me on and makes me feel like I'm the only woman in the world. Because he's patient and playful and makes me laugh.

A dildo can't do that.

I look at it in my hand, garishly pink, and toss it on the table as if it's suddenly caught fire. I hunt around for my phone, dragging it out from under some papers, my fingers shaking as I message him.

> Come and do me now!!!

My finger pauses over the send button, and I delete it after a couple of seconds. I can't do that. Not after I rejected him and essentially told him to grow up. I know in my gut that I'm the one who has to go to him. He's the one who's made all the moves. Who's put himself out there for me. It's my turn to do the same for him.

But if I go to him, it can't just be for sex – that's not fair either. I can't use him for that. Not when I know he wants more. I have to want more, too.

And I do. I do want more.

I think for a little. My pulse is bounding through my body so hard I can feel it in my fingers as they hover over the keyboard. Finally, I settle on something simple.

> Are you home?

I stare at the phone for long moments, willing for those three little dots to appear that tell me he's texting back. Suddenly they do, and my pulse edges up a little higher.

> In 39. Fixing sink. Why? You get a delivery you need a hand with?

I laugh, not expecting him to crack open the door for me so readily. We've texted a few times this past two weeks but mostly just *are you okay* and *how was your day/night/shift/gig*. He has to know this is not that. And yet he's chosen to be funny/sexy/bantery Danny and I could kiss him for being so magnanimous.

And that's exactly what I'm going to do. He's not Warren, who would still be sulking over my refusal to fall in with his plan. He's Danny.

I don't stop to think. I don't even stop to change my clothes or run a brush through my hair or put on lipstick. I have to see him – now. I have to talk to him now. And it's not like the man was put off by me looking like the Yeti on the day of the blizzard.

I run down four flights of steps. The door to thirty-nine is open and I stride in, not knocking or waiting for an invitation to enter. Ahead of me is Danny in his regulation jeans and T-shirt, his shoulders broad, his ass to die for as he bends over the sink.

My heart leaps. And not because of his ass, but because of the sense of rightness settling in my bones. 'Danny?'

He turns abruptly, his eyebrows raised, his frown turning into one of those slow-burn smiles that I feel deep in my soul, as well as other places, as I shut the door behind me and stalk towards him, my heart swelling, every cell trembling. *Gah!* This man – I've been such an idiot.

'You need it that bad, huh?'

I give a husky half laugh as my greedy gaze eats him up. Glancing at the huge wrench in his hand, I say, 'We're not talking about that, I hope.' Because it's so good to see him and flirt with him.

He chuckles, and those dimples... I want to lick those dimples. 'I don't think you can handle the wrench. Although...' He tips his chin at the tool bag. 'I do have my lucky screwdriver with me.'

'Lucky screwdriver?'

'Forever to be known as,' he murmurs with a grin.

The wrench makes a metallic scraping sound as Danny places it in the sink. His biceps shift nicely at the action, the tatts on his arms play peek-a-boo with the sleeves. His fingers wrap around the edge of the sink behind him as he rests his ass against it, too, his legs casually extended and crossed at the ankles.

I try not to look at soft denim cupping the very nice bulge nestled between his legs, and fail. But I manage to contain it to a brief glance. He smiles as he clocks my interest.

'Does Mrs Duffy know she has a billionaire fixing her sink?'

Another smile. 'I'm keeping that on the quiet for a bit longer.'

'Still trying to figure things out?'

He nods. 'I'm working on it. I have a lawyer. Bob's lawyer, actually. He's looking in to how I can help veterans. There's a lot of vacant inner-city buildings all over the country since the pandemic changed the way people work. We think we can use them for housing. And we're looking at covering any and all healthcare costs for veterans who are in need.'

I blink. Wow. 'Danny... that's...' I shake my head in wonder. 'Amazing.'

'Thanks to you for the kick up the ass.'

I laugh. 'You'd have figured it out in due course.' I shake my head again, thrilled at this outcome. 'Bob would have loved what you're doing.'

Danny gives a sad sort of smile as he nods. 'Yeah... I think he would have.' A rich streak of pride in his voice causes the skin on my arms to break out in goosebumps. 'We have other ideas.'

'We?'

'I've formed a board.' He laughs then like he can't quite believe it himself. 'With a few of Bob's military buddies. They're kind of a brains trust. We're kicking stuff around, exploring the possibilities.'

'I have some possibilities,' I offer tentatively.

Danny's blue eyes light up. 'Yeah?'

'A couple that would really complement what you're doing around veteran health.'

He quirks an eyebrow. 'Is that why you're here?'

He's looking at me intently now, like he's hoping it's not. Like he's hoping I'm here for reasons that don't involve his inheritance.

'No.' I shake my head.

My breath is suddenly thick as fog in my throat. I haven't really prepared a speech. I'd just run, needing to see him. This isn't like me at all – acting on impulse. But I haven't been me since I met Danny Colton and that had worried me, but actually, I realise now that I like myself better this way.

His smile grows bigger. 'Breathe, Doc.'

I give a half laugh at the absurdity of it, but at least it forces me to take a breath, and it bolsters me. 'I've come to say... yes.'

He cocks an eyebrow. 'To?' He's the epitome of laid-back cool, but I notice his knuckles turning white around the lip of the sink.

'Filling in my gaps.' A huge weight lifts from my shoulders as I say it and, bolstered even further, I press on. 'If that's still on offer.'

'Because of the dildo?' He laughs. 'If I'd known buying it for you was going to have this result, I'd have hand-delivered it. Two weeks ago.'

'No, not the dildo. Well, yes... but no.'

'Okay?'

'It was the catalyst. It got me thinking about the difference between a penis substitute and the real thing. Between a flesh-and-blood man and a silicon stand-in. Between a full life and half one. Between living and existing.'

'And you want to live?'

I nod. 'I do. And be loved. And love in return. I'm in love with you, Danny, and I'm sorry I panicked two weeks ago when you told me you loved me, but I was still running scared then.'

'And you're not now?' The question is surprisingly sober, as is Danny's demeanour – the answer is clearly important.

I shake my head. 'No. Because I realise I don't have to choose medicine or you. You're not Warren. You showed me I can have both. I just have to open myself up to it. So, here I am, opening myself to it. If you'll still have me.'

He grins, his serious expression melting as he grabs me. 'I thought you'd never ask.'

And then his mouth is on me, hot and urgent, and his hands are on me, hot and urgent, turning me, the sink digging into my lower back as he cages me between it and his body, his rapidly swelling cock grinding into the juncture of my legs. It's exactly where I want to be and what I want to be doing – kissing and loving on Danny Colton.

For as long as he'll have me.

Forever, I hope.

'Christ,' he mutters, tearing his mouth from mine. 'I want to rip open your shirt, turn you around, and fuck you from behind until you scream.'

My already shaky legs wobble some more as I half pant, half laugh. 'Sounds good.'

'Don't tempt me, Doc.'

I sigh. 'You're right, my timing sucks. I have to go back and study. But I have planned a break for twelve.' There's a clock hanging on the nearby wall. 'That's three hours.'

'Perfect,' he says and kisses me again until I'm moaning and shifting against him.

I break away this time. I really do need to get back to my books. 'I'll come to yours at twelve?'

'No.' He shakes his head. 'I'll come to you. I'll always come to you. Deal?'

His voice is all low and growly and so damn hot that I nod because I'm not sure I can find my voice right at this second.

'Text me when you stop for your break.' And he kisses me again, brief and hard, before stepping back a pace, far enough to release me from the cage of his body but close enough for me to still feel the tension in his frame. 'Now go.'

My entire body protests the move, and I think, *screw it*. I don't want to wait. 'Is Mrs Duffy around?'

He shakes his head. 'She nipped out for half an hour about fifteen minutes ago.'

Which gives me fifteen minutes, but I reckon I'm only going to need a couple. A surge of female power spurts through my veins, and I step forward and reclaim the distance he put between us, smiling at him as my hand slides to the button of his jeans.

'Doc.' He smiles back as he glances at my busy fingers, his frame relaxing into bemusement, but not for long, I hope. 'What are you doing?'

'I'm going to give you a blow job.'

He chuckles. 'I love it when you talk dirty.'

I yank his zipper down, and the tension returns to his body. He's not laughing now. 'What can I say? Being with you has been rather liberating, and I've missed...' I lean forward and press my lips to his ear and whisper, 'Sucking your cock.'

I sink to my knees.

'Oh... Jesus.' His hands grip the sides of his thighs as he stares down at me. 'I've created a monster.'

I smile as I reach inside his jeans and pull his erection free, wrapping my hands around it. A groan that sounds as if it was torn from his throat bubbles into the air and he makes a grab for the sink.

'Talking of monsters,' I mutter as I stare at his big, beautiful cock.

He laughs, but it cuts off as I lean forward and open my mouth over him. He groans, deep and long, and I'm vaguely aware of the muscle in his forearm bulging as he grips the sink harder. I don't pussyfoot around, I don't tease with my tongue and hands, I just go for it. I can dazzle him with technique some-time Mrs Duffy won't bust me on my knees giving the building super a blow job.

'Fuck... Holly... I love watching your mouth swallow me.'

I glance up to find him watching me, watching the spread of my lips as they plunge down his shaft. I take him as deep as I can while I look at him, and he grunts his pleasure. I do it again, my hand sliding to his ass, anchoring there, feeling his glute contract as his shaft disappears almost all the way behind my lips.

'Jesus,' he mutters and grabs for the sink with his other hand, his eyes shutting.

Mine do too, savouring the musky taste and the soapy smell of him, the thickness of him, the wet glide of his shaft between my lips, the wideness of my jaw as I take him deeper and deeper. His thighs are trembling. So are mine. And I'm hot and wet and slippery between my legs, and my nipples are stiff and raw from rubbing against the lace of my bra.

I know all I need to do is slip a hand between my legs and I'll fall apart. But this isn't about me. It's about Danny, about loving Danny, and power swells in my veins as he mutters something guttural and unintelligible. It goads me to stop and play for a bit when I know I shouldn't.

I pull off and I wait until his eyes flick open before I deliberately run the wet, plump head of his cock around my lips, snaking my tongue out, swiping it over the top, back and forth as he watches. I lick down the underside, his shaft brushing my cheek.

'Christ, that's hot,' he mutters, a rich, dark glitter coming into his eyes as his hand leaves the sink to bury itself in my hair, angling my head a little for him to thrust his hips and glide himself up and down my tongue, run himself around my lips.

'Open,' he says, and I open, my eyes glued on his as he pushes slowly into my mouth, right to the back, and I hold it there until I can't any longer, gagging a little just as he eases the pressure on my hair and the back of my throat.

He does it again, angling my head further, pushing in again. My eyes water, and saliva floods my mouth, but his eyes are practically rolling back in his head, and I hold still, watching him, watching his pleasure as his cock sits deeper this time even as my throat works against the stimulus.

He eases off again, and I smile up at him around the fullness of his shaft.

He smiles back as he untwists his hand from my hair and reluctantly shoves it back on the edge of the sink. He grunts, knowing we don't have time for the porn blow job version I really want to give him.

'Suck it.'

I don't need to be told twice. I shut my eyes then and suck. I suck hard and fast, my tongue swirling up and down his shaft as I go, and I have him breathing hard and trembling in less than a minute.

He groans, and my eyes flick open, meeting his as he says, 'Christ. I'm going to come.'

My heart rate spikes, and I moan around his cock, going harder and faster, digging my fingers into his ass.

'Ahh... Goddamn... fuuuck.'

His voice is a loud whisper as the first salty taste of him spills across my tongue. I moan and take him deep as he unloads. He grunts through his climax, his hands gripping the sink hard, his eyes shut, his face screwed into a mask of agony and ecstasy as he fights the urge to bellow his pleasure.

I suck him until there's nothing left, and he sags a little and opens his eyes. Slowly I slide off him and smile. He laughs and shakes his head. 'Fuck, Holly.' He pants a couple of times. 'I think I just saw God.'

I laugh, dizzy at the compliment, high on the taste of him, but only for a nanosecond as a key scrapes at the lock. 'Crap!' His eyes bug wide open. 'That's her.'

If it wasn't so serious it would be funny, the two of us frantically righting ourselves, straightening up, tucking ourselves away.

'Jesus.' His voice is a husky whisper as he looks at my mouth and shakes his head. 'You *look* like you've just been sucking cock.'

'Yeah? Well, you look like you've just *had* your cock sucked.'

His nostrils flare this time, but the door opens and Mrs Duffy enters. 'Sorry that didn't take as long as I thought,' she announces, halting her progress as soon as she notices me. 'Oh, hello, Holly dear.' She smiles. 'I didn't know Daniel had company.'

I cock an eyebrow at him. Daniel? Hmmm. I like it. 'No, I'm sorry, I'm...'

I'm what? The answer eludes me. I'm... just sucking Daniel's cock? I hadn't thought about how I was going to present us to other people. I was only just wrapping my head around there being an us. I panic for a second before I realise there's no need. I'm in love with Danny and I want to tell the world.

'Danny's my boyfriend. I was just checking how he was doing.'

And just like that, it's easy. So easy. Danny is my boyfriend. He makes everything so easy. Including loving him.

'Oh, how lovely,' the older woman beams. 'You two are perfect for each other.'

'I think so,' Danny agrees, dazzling the older woman with his dimples before turning to me. 'I'll see you at twelve?'

The promise in his eyes is unmistakable. Hell yes. 'Sure.'

He smiles and mouths, 'Be naked,' as Mrs Duffy turns away, and I smile too, my heart practically floating out of my chest knowing there's going to be a whole lot of naked times with Danny in my future.

And it starts at midday.

# EPILOGUE
## ONE YEAR LATER...

### *HOLLY AND DANNY PLAY DOCTOR*
#### *Danny*

It's just past two in the morning when my phone beeps. I only got back from a two-day board meeting in Reno at dinner time so I'm dead to the world, but I'm particularly attuned to the cymbal swell that is Holly's ringtone.

I reach for it before I'm even fully awake, squinting at the bright light from the screen to discover a message. We bought a place of our own a couple of months ago and though our lives are busy – I gave up the band now the housing project is picking up momentum and Holly's life is still ruled by her shifts – we are thriving as a couple.

> Are you awake?

I smile at the screen.

> I am now. Of course. Thinking about what I'm going to do to you in the morning when you get home.

Three dots appear as she types her reply. My dick twitches as I wait. It's not the first time she's woken me for some sexting, and I love how bold she gets when she doesn't have to say any of those words out loud. Although I have managed to corrupt her a lot this past year – she can be quite filthy when she has a mind to.

> Can't wait till then. Can you come see me now?

Can I get my ass out of bed, go to the hospital and do bad things to the woman I love? Fucking A I can – I'm already kicking off the sheet. But she doesn't have to know that. I smile as I tap my reply.

> Well... I'm very tired... would it be worth my while, Doc?

I send the message and throw the phone on the bed as I grab the chinos and T-shirt I'd stepped out of several hours ago and throw them on. When I'm dressed, I scoop the phone off the mattress.

On the screen is a titty pic. Holly's taken off her shirt and bra, slung her stethoscope around her neck, and snapped a picture. God, I love this woman. My mouth waters at her perky mocha nipples, and my dick roars to life.

> I'll be there in ten.

I stride out of the bedroom and grab the keys off the counter. The phone chimes again.

> Take elevator to eleven. Go through push doors.
> Ignore closed signs. I'll be in room three.

I frown at the screen. I thought the hospital only had ten floors? It's a mysterious request, and my blood stirs. More dots dance on the screen before another text appears.

> Message me when you're pulling into parking lot.

My hand shakes in anticipation. I don't know what she has planned for me and I don't care – only one thing matters, and I tap it out now.

> Be naked.

* * *

I'm pushing past the closed signs on eleven in twelve minutes. A dark corridor stretches ahead of me. The only source of light is a smudge on the linoleum floor down the other end and I head towards it, my legs eating up the distance, my groin wound tighter than a guitar string, my blood thick and hot in my veins.

The rooms on either side count down from twenty, and all the doors are open as I pass. They're full of ancient-looking equipment – from beds to IV poles to all kinds of machinery. The corridor is also lined with discarded gear. It must be the place equipment comes to die.

The room the light comes from is number three, and my pulse picks up as I turn into it and pause on the threshold. There's more equipment crammed in here, but right in the back corner, a light is shining. It's a free-standing lamp. The light source is at the end of an angled arm, which is currently hovering over the top of what looks like one of those narrow examination beds.

It's hard to tell properly from here. The bed has been placed diagonally in the corner, and all I can see is the underside of the top half, which has been raised to almost ninety degrees. Like the rest of the equipment I've seen here, it doesn't look new. The metal is pockmarked, and it seems to be of very basic construction, like something from a black-and-white photograph.

Holly's not here. 'Doc?'

Suddenly, a fuzz of dark hair appears at the top of the raised portion of the bed. The head turns, and Holly is peeping out over the edge. The usual flood of emotion I experience whenever I see her hits me in the chest.

'I thought you'd never get here.'

There's impatience in her voice and that note of huskiness I've come to know so well. She's really turned on. My cock stiffens.

'How long have you been lying there waiting for me?' I ask as I pick a path through the equipment. All I can see is from her nose up, but I just know she's naked over there, and it suddenly feels like a hundred miles away.

'Too long. I almost started without you.'

I laugh as I reach the raised end. She's turned back and all I can see is the top of her head again, so I walk around. The sight that greets me stops my breath.

She's lying on the narrow bed, naked except for her stethoscope. Her tits are high and full, her nipples hard and flushed with arousal, and I wonder if she's been playing with them while she waited. Her dark hair is in some kind of updo. A few tendrils have escaped and brush her neck, but my eyes fall to the bell of the stethoscope, brushing her cleavage like it had in the titty pic. One of the earpieces kisses the mocha circle surrounding her nipple.

But the most fascinating part is the way Holly's legs are positioned. I walk to the end of the bed to get a closer look. They're primly together but bent at the knees, her calves resting in mounted stirrups, which are attached to a slide bar just under where the mattress abruptly ends. Her bare ass hangs over the edge a little.

Christ... this is like every sick fantasy I've ever had, rolled into one.

'I'm so pleased you could make it, Doctor,' she says, all high and breathy, some of which I suspect is deliberate, some of it not. She toys with the earpieces of the stethoscope. 'I have this terrible ache between my legs.'

Slowly, with some squeaking of metal, the stirrups separate. As do her legs. In seconds she is wide open, her legs well and truly out of the way, and I'm staring at her almost-bare pussy, her inner thighs glistening in the light from the lamp behind.

'Holy fuck,' I whisper. My cock is so hard now I'm pretty sure it's entered a state of rigor mortis.

'Oh, hurry, Doctor, please. The pain is getting worse.'

I blow out an unsteady breath as my gaze treks up her body. She's fucking gorgeous and she's all mine.

* * *

*Holly*

I can barely breathe as Danny's hot gaze brands me as his. My pussy – yes, pussy – pulses at the heat in those blue eyes, and I suppress the urge to squirm at the sudden, delicious gleam that enters them.

'Never fear, Miss Vincent,' he says, his voice deeper and gruffer than normal. 'I'm sure I can cure it.'

My heart trips as he slips into his role. 'Oh, could you?' I toy with the earpieces of the stethoscope, and a hot wave of wantonness rolls through my belly as his eyes zero in on the movement. The urge to arch my back rides me hard, but I suppress it as one of my fingers accidentally brushes my nipple.

'I'd be ever so grateful if you could, Doctor. I can pay you.'

'We'll talk about payment after,' he says, dragging his gaze from my chest as he steps into the space between my legs I created when I spread them.

'Yes. Thank you, Doctor.' His eyes trek a path down my inner thighs now, and I swear it smoulders in their wake.

'Do you have a fever down there?' he asks in such a clinically detached way I'm glad I'm already horizontal. His gaze stops when it reaches the juncture of my thighs, and he takes his time examining it.

My breathing is thick as soup in my lungs. 'It's very hot down there.'

He nods. 'I'm going to have to take your temperature.'

'But... you don't have your thermometer with you.'

He raises his gaze to mine and smiles. Clinically, cynically, like the doctor he's pretending to be, not laid back like my Danny. 'Did you know, Miss Vincent, that the male penis is the most accurate thermometer in the world?'

My thighs tremble. 'No... I didn't, Doctor.'

'Oh yes.' He rips his zip down. It's loud in the silence of the long-deserted ward eleven. My breath hitches. 'Just hold still now, okay? Let's find out just how hot you are.'

I catch only a glimpse of his straining cock before he slowly inserts it inside of me. He doesn't put on a condom. We both went through testing months ago.

His eyes shut briefly, and so do mine. My hand falls from the stethoscope, and I bite back a moan as his girth splits me right up the middle, and he settles himself to the hilt. We've done this hundreds of times this last year, and I don't think I'll ever get used to this moment as his eyes, a hot tub of desire, flick open and capture mine.

It takes my breath away every time.

'Oh yesss.' His voice is a low hiss. 'You're very hot. You definitely have a fever.'

I pant, shift against the mattress, and bite my lip to stop from crying out. 'Is that bad, Doctor?'

'It can be.'

I crinkle my brow in concern. 'Is there a cure?'

'Yes.' He does that clinical nod again, like his dick isn't still sitting hard and high inside me being used as a human thermometer. 'There are a couple of options, Miss Vincent.'

'Which one would you recommend, Doctor?'

'The internal application of male semen is the one I usually suggest.'

I suck in a breath, loving how Danny is getting into this. It's beyond my wildest imaginings. When I messaged him, I just needed to see him, needed to feel him inside me, a quick fuck somewhere quiet because he's been away and it's been such a torment for my body that I just can't seem to get enough of him.

But this... this is freaking epic.

'Okay.' I toy with the stethoscope again, my heart just about leaping out of my chest I'm so freaking turned on. 'Would you be willing to supply that for me?'

'Of course.' He gives me a stern look, as if I'm questioning his Hippocratic Oath. 'I am duty bound to provide for my patients.'

'I'll pay whatever.'

'That's not important for now. What's critically important is that you must lie very still. You mustn't move or shift or cry out, even if, during the process, you climax. It's better for the treatment if you do, but for the most effective outcome, the semen must have a passive entry into your body. Do you under-stand, Miss Vincent?'

Oh fuck... I love him and I hate him all at once. I'm probably going to have the most intense orgasm of my life, and he wants me to totally internalise it.

If he thinks I won't get my revenge for this, he's wrong.

'Well?' His voice might be low, but it cracks like a whip, and my internal muscles clamp around him hard.

'Yes, Doctor.'

'Good.' He nods, satisfied, and if it wasn't for his cock jammed inside me and the tremble of his hands as they slide down my thighs, I could almost believe he really was just doing his job.

'Now, hold on to the sides of the couch, Miss Vincent. And I'll begin.'

I grip the sides and bite down on the gasp that pushes against my vocal cords as he withdraws. A ghost of a smile touches his mouth, but it's gone again and then he hammers me. I was expecting him to tease me slowly with his cock until I disobey him and beg for him to finish the job. But Danny knows how quickly I can be called away, and he's obviously not taking any chances.

My tits rock and the stethoscope bounces as he drives into me, and he doesn't take his eyes off them. He just thrusts and thrusts and thrusts, my position in the stirrups just the right angle for him to hit my G spot over and over and over, and he doesn't even need to touch my clit. He's building quickly, and I'm building with him, fighting the urge to move and speak every step of the way.

Fighting the urge to arch my back and lift my hips to meet each stroke. To twist and tweak my nipples. To pant and gasp and moan as ripples spread outwards from my belly button and pulse through me. My eyes widen as the climax roars up from the base of my spine, innervating every inch of my body.

I cut off the threatening cry, sucking air in and out through my nostrils so loud it sounds like a tornado's landed. My heart races like a train, and my body trembles, fibrillating against the mattress as I deny it the movement it craves.

He watches me fight the powerful dictates of my orgasm as he reaches his own. But he doesn't come quiet. Oh no. He groans and mutters, 'Fuck, fuck, fuck,' as he buries deep and empties inside me, pulsing in and out in small, precise movements which make me want to bite and holler and scream but which I suck up, morphing my orgasm into an intensity that takes me to a whole other plane.

When it's finally over, I am wrecked. How on earth I'm going to go back to the ER to work, I have no idea.

'Good job, Miss Vincent.' Danny, whose breathing has just about recovered, pulls out, and I do moan this time as he zips up. 'I recommend internal application of semen morning and night for the next week.'

If I wasn't so spaced out I'd laugh. So I just say, 'Yes, Doctor.'

He pats me on the knee then – on the freaking knee – and says, 'I'll see you in a few hours for your next treatment.'

And he leaves.

I blink, amazed anew at Danny's ability to recover so quickly, even though I shouldn't be after all this time. I'm lying spread-eagled in stirrups, possibly forever, if I can't get my legs to cooperate, and he's walking away. I don't even know my own name at the moment, and he's walking upright, the sound of his boots on the linoleum gradually fading.

There are two things I do know.

Number one – I'm going to love that man forever. And number two – morning can't come soon enough.

\* \* \*

## MORE FROM AMY ANDREWS

Another book from Amy Andrews, is available to order now here: https://mybook.to/AmyBrandNewBackAd

# ACKNOWLEDGMENTS

This book started out as a much shorter novella written in 2018 which I have significantly re-edited to expand the story. Be assured though, it's still as filthy as it was back when it was first written ☺

Big thanks to Megan Haslam from Boldwood Books for welcoming this dirtier side of Amy *and* knowing when to rein her in a little. Thanks also to the entire Boldwood staff who are awesome at what they do – it's a privilege to be part of Team BW.

Thanks also to my agent, Jill Marsal.

As ever, extra special thanks to you, the reader. It's nice to know that this thing I do, toiling away every day at my keyboard, is embraced by complete strangers all around the world, who only ask for a HEA and then trust me to do the rest.

You guys really do rock! Big love to you all xxx

# ABOUT THE AUTHOR

**Amy Andrews** is an award-winning, USA Today best-selling, Australian author of over ninety contemporary romances.

Download your exclusive bonus content from Amy Andrews here:

Follow Amy on social media here:

facebook.com/AmyAndrewsAuthor
x.com/AmyAndrewsbooks
instagram.com/amyandrewsbooks
tiktok.com/@amyandrewsbooks

# ALSO BY AMY ANDREWS

# Boldwood
# EVER AFTER

xoxo

JOIN BOLDWOOD'S
**ROMANCE
COMMUNITY**
FOR SWEET AND
SPICY BOOK RECS
WITH ALL YOUR
FAVOURITE
TROPES!

SIGN UP TO OUR
NEWSLETTER

HTTPS://BIT.LY/BOLDWOODEVERAFTER

# Boldwood

Boldwood Books is an award-winning fiction publishing company seeking out the best stories from around the world.

**Find out more at www.boldwoodbooks.com**

Join our reader community for brilliant books, competitions and offers!

Follow us
@BoldwoodBooks
@TheBoldBookClub

Sign up to our weekly deals newsletter

https://bit.ly/BoldwoodBNewsletter

www.ingramcontent.com/pod-product-compliance
Lightning Source LLC
Chambersburg PA
CBHW011801010726
47497CB00012B/3227